MW00476164

BLUE RIDGE BREAKDOWN

RACHEL HANNA

CHAPTER 1

*A*va Monroe held onto the steering wheel of her old truck like her life depended on it, and it probably did. Her knuckles were turning white. Outside, a snowstorm had transformed the world around her into a blur of white and shadow. The flakes were falling so thickly that it seemed like she would be swallowed up at any moment. Like in front of her, there would be nothing and everything at the same time.

Why she had chosen to drive her vintage red truck for this trip, she had no idea. It was something she cherished. Her father had bought the ratty shell of a truck when she was just a baby, and after he passed, her grandfather decided to restore it in honor of his late son. Ava had helped him when she was just twelve years old, learning all about old trucks in the process. When she'd taken off and left town, the truck was one thing she wasn't willing to leave behind. Now, she was regretting that decision a bit.

She'd left the main road behind a long time ago, trying to put as much distance between herself and the situation she was fleeing. All of it felt like a surreal dream that she was trying to wake up from but just kept getting worse. Her brain seemed to want to roll the events leading up to this over and over in her mind, but she tried to push it away.

Somehow she found herself driving up a mountain that she wasn't expecting. Of course, when a person flees their life, they don't really tend to look at a map. She just wanted to go, get out of there as quickly as possible, and that seemed to have led to a really poor decision. She had never driven in snow, and she certainly hadn't ever driven over a mountain, but now she found herself doing both. The tires crunched against the snow-packed road, and it was the only sound in the otherwise silent snowstorm. It truly felt like she was the last person on earth. The quiet was deafening.

She questioned every decision she'd made in her life in the last couple of years and certainly the one she had made that morning when she decided to just drive. Visibility was almost at zero, and the road seemed like more of a path now. Everything disappeared just a few feet ahead of her vehicle.

She looked down at her fuel gauge and realized that she was running dangerously low on gas. She had a sinking feeling in her stomach.

"Just a little further," she said to herself and the truck, hoping to find a place that she could pull over and figure out her next steps. But the last thing she wanted to do was pull over on a snowy mountain. There was no telling what could happen to her there. There were no other cars passing her. In fact, she hadn't seen another person since she got on the mountain, probably because they were smarter than her and stayed home.

Suddenly, as she turned one of the curves as slowly as possible, her truck lurched. A hidden patch of ice sent it skidding off the narrow road and into a snowbank on the side. She didn't have to worry about anybody coming up behind her and running into her because there was no other traffic. Again, she was the only genius who would end up in this mess. Just like her life. A big mess.

Her engine stalled and left her sitting in silence, except for the sound of her own ragged breathing.

She kept trying to crank the truck over and over again, but it refused to start.

The storm seemed to be getting heavier. Mother Nature certainly didn't seem to care about her plight. She wrapped her arms around herself as the cold started seeping into the truck. She looked over at her beloved boxer, Millie, who was still sleeping peacefully in the passenger seat next to her, as if nothing was going on. That dog could never be rattled. She'd had her for three years now and she was her best friend and closest companion, the one who would never judge her for all the silly mistakes she'd made.

Now, as she sat alone with her truck broken down on the side of a mountain during a snow-storm, Ava wondered if this was going to be her last day on earth. She didn't have any food. She was only wearing a sweater and had a lightweight jacket under her purse in the passenger floorboard. Panic started to set in as the gravity of the situation became clear. She was all alone, as usual. She had no cell service, no way to call anybody for help, and she was certain that it was many miles to the nearest town. She took in a deep breath and pulled her sweater tightly around her. She needed to think. She had to come up with a plan, but as she looked out into the snow swirling in front of her, she couldn't help but wonder if she had escaped one nightmare only to find herself trapped in another one.

MADELINE WAS in her favorite place on earth - inside of her cozy cabin overlooking the Blue Ridge Mountains with snow falling outside. She snuggled up next to Brady, pulling the blanket tighter around them as they sat in front of the crackling fire. They had been snuggled up like this for well over an hour, and she was hesitant to move because she was so comfortable and warm.

He turned and looked over at her. "It's hard to believe," he said, "after everything that happened - the fire, the loss - we're finally going to have a place to call home again." He squeezed her hand. After losing his family home in a fire a few months ago, Brady was very excited to have his sister and niece with him in a brand new house on their family property.

"I've seen the work that you've put into it, Brady. Every nail, every board. It's not just going to be your house. It's going to be a place that stands as proof of your strength and your resilience. Jasmine and Anna are very lucky to have you."

He laughed under his breath. "Well, you know I couldn't have done it without you. You've encouraged me the entire way, even on the days where I wanted to quit. You helped me keep going so that I could have a home that will stand the test of time. I can't believe we're just a couple of weeks away from moving in. Jasmine has already started planning a garden, and Anna has been trying to pick the color for her room."

She leaned back into him, resting her head on his shoulder. "It's going to be a wonderful, beautiful start to this new year, a new beginning for all of you." They sat there silently listening to the fire crackle, the only sound in the room for a few minutes.

"You know, I was thinking."

"Thinking what?"

"Well, once the house is finished, maybe we could have some family dinners there from time to time."

She smiled. "Of course. Just because we have two different homes doesn't mean that we can't go back and forth between them. That's double the blessing, right?"

"Yeah. And it's not like we live far apart," he said, laughing.

She often wondered if he thought about the future, their future. Would they ever get married? And if they did, where would they live? She loved her home overlooking the mountains, and he would certainly love his home right there on the farm. It would be a hard choice, but certainly not something she had to think about anytime soon. They hadn't been together that long, and Madeline wasn't somebody who rushed into anything. She was happy where they were right now.

"And you know that I think of your family as my family, and I hope you think the same about my mom."

Brady nodded. "Of course. We are both very blessed to have everyone in our lives like we do."

They looked out the window with the snowstorm raging. Within the walls of Madeline's cabin, there was only warmth. As they sat by the fire continuing to discuss the plans for the cabin and all the great things that would happen there, Madeline knew she was exactly where she was meant to be.

CLEMMY LIKED to think of herself as a risk-taker, but as she watched the snow fall harder and harder outside the windows of her bookstore, she wondered if she had made the wrong decision. Away With Words was her baby. She loved it more than just about anything, except for her grown son, who she rarely got to see. It was the thing that got her out of bed each morning and excited her about the day. She loved meeting new people who came into the store and also interacting with her regular customers. She loved to read, so in her downtime between customers, she would always grab a book from one of the shelves and escape into its pages.

But right now, she found herself stuck in a moment of indecision. Should she go ahead and close early and get home before the snow got too bad, or take her chances later when it was starting to get dark? She knew what the decision should be, but that wasn't the one she made.

Instead, she went and sat back on her tall stool behind the cash register and looked out over the beautiful town square. She had a wonderful view of the snow falling in front of the red brick courthouse. People were still driving, albeit slow. She knew there might be some ice later, and she had to get home before that happened, of course. But as a mountain woman, she was pretty accustomed to driving in the snow from time to time. Although she loved her home, she also loved being at the bookstore. It was her refuge, even on her stormiest days.

She looked at the clock as another hour passed and felt a little sense of unease in her stomach. Maybe she should have closed earlier. But what if somebody needed to come get some books before the snowstorm kept them inside for a few days? The streets of Jubilee were usually bustling with activity, but now it was almost eerily silent, with just the occasional vehicle passing in front of her shop. The foot traffic was much less today as the weather worsened. She watched the snowflakes, large and relentless, as they blanketed the world outside in white. Suddenly, the shops didn't look like themselves anymore, as they were obscured by the blinding snow falling harder and harder.

"Goodness, I should have seen this coming," she muttered to herself, looking at the snow accumulating on the windowsills across the way. The weather forecast had not said it was going to be quite this bad, although it was labeled a significant snowstorm. Now she wondered if she was going to be able to get home at all.

Thankfully, she had an area in the back room

where she could sleep if she needed to. It wasn't comfortable, and it definitely wasn't her first choice, but she would do it if it meant that she would be safe. The bookstore was warm and would be a perfectly fine place to spend the night if she had to, but her intention was to get home, make a big pot of vegetable soup, and sit by the fire for the rest of the night. She decided that she would stay another hour, maybe two, before she would close up and head home.

Her thoughts were interrupted by the chime of the door. Just as she suspected, one of her regular customers had come in to load up with books so they could sit by the fire and read them as the snowflakes fell. She was distracted by the conversation, which was a good thing because she didn't want to sit around and worry about getting home later. Instead, she would do what she always did, dive headfirst into the fictional world sitting in the book in front of her, and make real-world decisions later.

Ava's breath fogged up the inside of the truck, showing just how cold it was getting outside. As the snowstorm raged, her gas light had been on for at least the last three miles before she had run into the snowbank. It was a constant reminder of her precarious situation. She pulled her jacket ever tighter, wishing that she had brought a heavy coat. She had assumed wrongly that she would be in her truck with a heater all the way to her destination, even though she didn't know where her destination was. She had just packed up her things and started driving. She figured when she found the place she was supposed to be, maybe she would feel it. Maybe she would get some sort of feeling in her bones.

But right now, all she felt was cold and scared. Her phone was the last lifeline she had to the outside world, but there were no bars, no service. She kept checking it hoping that somehow, some way a signal would come through. She decided that maybe she should try one more time, but step out of the truck. Maybe if she walked a few feet ahead up the mountain, she could get that one bar of signal that she needed.

She carefully cracked open the door, and the biting howl of the wind got louder as it found its way inside the truck. She stuck her arm out into the snowstorm, her phone clutched tightly in her hand, which was quickly turning red, her eyes squinting against the snowflakes as they hit her in the face. In just that little moment, the world inside the truck went from being a sanctuary to a whirlwind of cold and chaos.

Her dog Millie, who was normally calm and composed, got startled by the sudden influx of the cold air, or maybe she sensed Ava's desperation, and she sprang into action. With a suddenness that even took Ava by surprise, she pushed past her legs and darted out into the snow-covered forest beside them. "Millie! No, Millie!" Ava cried out her voice dripping in panic.

She jumped completely out of the truck at this point, chasing after her beloved dog. As soon as she stepped all the way out, the intensity of the storm hit her with a full force biting at her exposed skin, blurring her vision.

"Millie, please come back here!" she shouted, but she didn't even know where her words were going. Everything was getting swallowed up by the storm. She was insignificant against the white expanse. Everywhere she turned looked exactly the same. She had no idea where her dog had run, and she could barely see her bright red truck even a few steps away. She called out one more time, but there was no sign of her. The thought that her dog could be gone, lost to the snowstorm, frightened and alone, was a blow that left her feeling completely isolated and desperate. She knew she couldn't stay outside the truck for much longer or risk hypothermia.

She jumped back in the truck, shaking from the cold, hoping against hope that she could warm back up again. She looked out her windshield and through every window trying to see her dog in the whiteout, hoping for any sign of her, but there was none. Now, she was truly alone. She didn't even have Millie for comfort.

Tears welled up in her eyes, and she felt a sharp ache in her stomach from Millie's absence. She leaned her forehead against the steering wheel, feeling the weight of the whole situation closing in on her. The storm was showing no signs of letting up, and now her dog was gone, facing a long, cold night. She wondered if she was going to survive this.

BRADY AND MADELINE decided that there was nothing better to do during a snowstorm than to invite more people over to enjoy the coziness of sitting by the fire, watching the snow fall outside. Madeline's cabin was nestled amidst the thick blanket of snow, and it glowed from within.

Laughter and conversation filled the air as Jasmine and Anna joined them. Brady and his sister had become closer and closer since she had come back to town, and he adored his niece, Anna.

The storm outside made the cabin's warmth all the more inviting as it provided a safe haven against the chill of wintertime. Madeline had put extra blankets and pillows around the living room and, as the fire cracked in the hearth, conversation flowed. The night wore on as they watched Anna, who asked questions about pretty much every topic under the sun.

"So, Grandma Eloise," she began, "tell us more about Burt. Are you in love?" Anna made a kissy face.

Everybody giggled. Eloise was obviously caught off guard, and her face blushed a shade deeper than the red in the wine that she sipped.

"Oh, well, Burt is a very kind man," she stammered, a smile starting to spread across her face. "He has a wonderful way with animals, as you all know. It's quite remarkable, really."

Madeline laughed under her breath watching her mother try to navigate this unexpected question. "I think he has a way with more than just animals. I seem to remember at the park that he had a certain way of charming my mother, as well," she teased.

"It's good to see that you're enjoying your new life, Eloise," Brady said, with a gentler tone. "I've always said that Jubilee has a way of bringing people together. Old Burt's been at that park for as long as I can even remember, taking care of the animals. He loves to feed the squirrels and the birds, and it's nice to see that he is getting some companionship, too."

Eloise smiled broadly. "It's been a very pleasant surprise. Life in Jubilee is full of those, it seems. Burt has been able to show me some of the best spots at the park. He's told me stories about his youth, about the town. It's truly been lovely," she said.

Jasmine leaned forward. "It sounds like there might be some romance in the air for you, Eloise. Jubilee is a magical place, isn't it? First Madeline and Brady. Now you."

Eloise waved her hand. "Oh, I don't know about all that. I'm pretty old for romance."

Brady winked at her. "You're never too old for romance, especially in Jubilee."

CHAPTER 2

*A*va had never seen such thick snow. The flakes looked like giant cotton balls as they fell from the sky, obscuring her view of just about everything. The snowstorm seemed to be intensifying, and she wrapped her arms around herself tightly, staring out the windshield.

She had to find her dog. It was the only comfort she had these days, but the world around her had turned into an unrecognizable landscape. Everything was white on white. She couldn't even make out the trees anymore.

Still, she couldn't let Millie be out there alone. If she died out in the forest, then Ava wanted to be right next to her. She stepped out of the truck one more time.

"Millie!" she yelled, her voice cracking as she shouted. It was like she was yelling into a vacuum. There was nothing there, yet everything was there. Her breath formed clouds of vapor that dissipated quickly, as if the cold air sucked them up.

She walked from one side of the truck to the other, looking into the dense forest, hoping that she would see her dog running toward her like one of those emotional commercials where a soldier returns home, but no such luck.

The cold was biting at her face, and the wind was whipping through her minimal clothing, finding every little gap to chill her skin. She realized tears were streaming down her reddened cheeks, and it felt like her teardrops were freezing to her skin. Panic and fear started to rise within her, not only for her own safety, but for Millie's. She knew her dog was not equipped for these kinds of harsh conditions. After all, she enjoyed sitting on her fluffy pillow at home right next to her mom, Ava, while she worked. Boxers weren't known for a lot of body fat, and Millie was lean. She had no padding to keep her warm for long. Every passing minute increased the danger for both of them.

Ava called out one more time, her voice becoming desperate, "Millie, please girl, come back!"

But the storm seemed to swallow up her pleas, leaving her feeling like she was more isolated than she'd ever been in her life. Like she was the only person on earth.

She stood there for a moment, her heart pounding in her chest, and listened for any kind of sound she could hear over the howling of the wind. There was nothing. There was no movement in the forest, no barking, just the relentless storm that didn't seem to care it had swallowed up her dog. After a few moments, she realized that her search was futile, and that she was at great risk if she stayed outside any longer. If she let herself pass away in the snowy depths beneath her, then her dog certainly wouldn't survive.

Ava's survival instincts finally kicked in. She knew that she needed to preserve what little body heat she had left, and being outside in the middle of the storm was making her tired. She looked one more time out into the white abyss, hoping that Millie would be standing there, wagging her tail, ready to run back to the truck. No such luck.

Ava turned and went back to her truck. She shut the door quickly, as she fumbled with the handle to get in. Once she finally managed to get inside, the truck was relatively warm, but it was a small comfort against the cold that had now settled into her bones. She slammed the door shut, stopping the wind from coming in, but not the sound of her own sobs.

She sat in the truck surrounded by the snow, which was something she used to think was so beautiful. Not anymore. It felt like a death sentence. She felt such a profound sense of helplessness. She had always considered herself to be such a good dog mom, but she had let Millie run off into the forest during the worst snowstorm she'd ever seen.

She wrapped her arms around herself again, trying to generate some kind of warmth, rubbing her upper arms as fast as she could. All she could think about was Millie. She had such turmoil inside of her when she had driven up the mountain in the first place, and now that was just intensified. As the snow piled up on her truck even more, she leaned her head against the window, the cold glass against her skin a harsh reminder of her reality. She sent up a silent prayer for Millie's safety and for her own. She thought about the bond they had, and she hoped to one day see her sweet little face again. But right now, all she could do was hope and try to survive.

IT IS interesting that when you're in a life and death situation, time seems to pass in a different way. Like you can't tell whether it's been a few minutes or a few hours. That's what Ava was finding as sleep tried to wrap itself around her with its seductive and dangerous lull.

In some moments, she would find herself in a state between dreaming and awake. She'd imagine things that weren't there, or maybe they were? It all felt so surreal. Sometimes, it felt almost peaceful, and it was those times that scared her most.

It got darker and darker outside. She had never been to the Blue Ridge Mountains, and certainly not stuck on the side of one of those mountains, but the darkness here was something like she'd never seen. She was used to the city with streetlights and cars honking. There was no sound here except for the howling of the wind, and there was certainly nothing to look at.

She couldn't see anything. She was just sitting in complete and total darkness like she was underground in some kind of cave. Her fuel gauge had been on empty for a while now, and the last of the engine's warmth had dissipated into the frigid air that was surrounding the truck. She knew that if she fell asleep now under these conditions, that she would not wake up. The exhaustion from the emotional turmoil in her life the last few days mixed with the physical chill outside made it very hard to stay awake. It made it very hard to want to keep going. After all, did she even have any hope?

There was nobody around. No houses, no other cars had passed. She couldn't move out of her small little space. There was nowhere to go, no one to ask for help. Maybe she should just realize that this was the last day of her life, maybe the last hour.

Her thoughts drifted from the immediate need to survive to thinking about the people who had shaped her life. Maybe this was that thing where your life flashes before your eyes right before you die. Although, she'd thought it would be a much quicker thing. When someone said flashed, she assumed it was a very quick little video, and then you were gone. This seemed much slower.

She thought about her mom who had always been strong and resilient. Ava could hear her voice, a soothing presence in the midst of the storm. "You're stronger than you know," her mom would say in a situation like this. Ava tried to hang on to that.

The thought of her mom finding out about her current predicament made her feel so regretful. The choices that she'd made in the last few months were not something her mother was proud of. She'd tried to warn her several times, but Ava didn't listen, and now she felt terribly sorry that her mother was going to hear about her passing away alone on the side of a mountain without even her dog sitting beside her. Her mother had always tried to teach her not to run away from her problems, but to stand up and face them.

Instead, Ava felt terrible that she had done just that. Run away. Not faced anything. Tried to get out of the situation by avoidance, which had been her pattern for as long as she could remember. Although, she wondered what other people would've done when they realized they were trapped in a situation like hers. Running had seemed the only way to survive and have any chance at a normal life.

Then she thought about her dad, who had been gone since she was seven years old. He had passed away in a work accident all those years ago, but he was never truly absent from her life. She had memories of him that were a mix of very vivid moments, and then the idealized image that one tends to create when they've lost someone so soon. He had been her hero, the man who could do no wrong in her eyes, and no other man had ever lived up to him. Ava remembered the way that he would lift her onto his shoulders and make her feel like she was on top of the world.

She thought if he was here right now, that he would be disappointed in her, in these decisions that had led to this moment. The moment that she was probably going to leave this world. She could almost hear him, although she didn't really remember his voice exactly. He would chide her gently for not thinking things through, for letting fear dictate her actions and put her in such a dangerous situation.

Ava believed in heaven, and she hoped she was going there. Maybe she'd get to see her dad again. That was a small comfort, but it was something to hold on to right now.

The reality of the situation, the running away from a life that felt more like a prison than a choice, from a future that terrified her almost as much as the storm outside, was a weight that she couldn't shake off. She had thought she was doing the right thing by saving herself from making a mistake that was too big to undo. But now she was rethinking that decision. Maybe she should have just gone through with it. Maybe she should have just settled. She wondered if this running away had been worth it.

She blinked away the tears as she stared out into

the darkness. The thought of her mom receiving news of her disappearance or her possible death, or having her own father's memory tarnished by her final, stupid, reckless decision was so painful that it enveloped her.

"I'm sorry," she whispered into the darkness. An apology her parents would never hear, of course, and maybe an apology to herself for ending up in this situation.

She tried to summon some resolve to survive, to not let this be the end of her story, but it felt like a flickering candle that was slowly dying. She tried and tried to try to stay awake, to fight against the sleep that was trying to take her. She forced her eyes open as much as she could. She didn't want to give up just yet, but she was starting to lose her resolve.

MADELINE HAD NEVER SEEN SUCH a snowstorm. As the snow swirled around outside and she looked out the window to the winter wonderland beyond, she saw Geneva wrapped in a thick woolen shawl being careful about her steps coming down the driveway. She couldn't believe Geneva was walking out in this snow.

She swung the door open and noticed that she was carrying a large, steaming pot of what was probably her famous vegetable soup. As she got closer to the front door, Madeline could smell the aroma and the promise of comfort and warmth.

"What in the world are you doing out here, you crazy woman?" Madeline said laughing.

Geneva chuckled under her breath. "I've lived in these mountains my whole life. Don't you think I can navigate a little snow?"

Madeline took the pot from Geneva. "I don't think this is a little snow. Get inside before you freeze to death."

Geneva waved her hand, like walking out in the snow was nothing. "I wouldn't miss hanging out with all of you during this snowstorm for anything. Do you think I want to sit over there all by myself?"

"Well, we're glad you're here," Brady said, walking over and giving her a hug. "I would've hated to have seen you frozen like a Popsicle laying out in the driveway."

She laughed, "I wouldn't have frozen. I had a nice hot pot of soup. I thought I would bring it over because there's no better way to ride out a snowstorm than with our bellies full."

Madeline's kitchen soon filled with the savory

smell of Geneva's soup. She got out several bowls and started filling them up for everybody. They all settled at the kitchen table with their bowls of steaming soup in front of them and some leftover cornbread that Madeline had. Nothing felt more comforting than a moment like this. Looking out over the Blue Ridge mountains, which were covered in snow, watching huge flakes fall.

The only way that they could even see the mountains was because the moon was so bright tonight, but it was still quite dark out in the woods.

"I still can't believe you would come over here in the pitch black darkness," Madeline said.

"Again, I've been here my whole life, and you live right next door," Geneva said shaking her head, "You're too dramatic. I think it's because you're an author."

"Well, next time it'd be great if you would just give me a phone call just the same. We could have come helped you."

Geneva stopped eating and stared at her. "You're treating me like I'm an old woman, and I'm not an old woman."

Madeline's mouth dropped, "I didn't mean to sound like I was saying…."

Geneva started laughing. "Oh, I'm just messing

with you. I am an old woman. That much is obvious. I see myself in the mirror every morning. But what I'm trying to say is that I'm not an invalid. I can handle things."

Eloise spoke up. "I know these young people think that we can't do things, and we *can* do things."

Madeline looked at her. "Excuse me, but didn't you arrive at my house just a few weeks ago because you couldn't do anything due to knee pain and needing surgery?"

Eloise shrugged her shoulders. "I could have gotten help if I wanted to. Maybe I just wanted to come see my daughter."

Madeline rolled her eyes and then laughed. "Okay, let's just say that's the truth."

"Ladies, ladies," Brady said, holding up his hands. "This is a nice moment. Let's not ruin it by getting into an argument."

Madeline looked over at him, "We're not getting into an argument. We're just being silly. That's all." Once everybody was finished eating their soup, Madeline felt like she didn't want the evening to end. "How about a game? Something to keep our minds off the storm?" She walked over and pulled a board game off the shelf.

"Nobody wants to play a board game," Eloise said.

"Well then, what kind of game do you want to play?"

"I don't know. Something where we don't have to think a whole lot. It's too cold to think."

"Mom, sit by the fire if you're cold," Madeline said pointing. Eloise walked over and sat on the end of the loveseat that was closest to the fire. "Let me see what other kind of game we might can play," Madeline said, walking over to her shelf.

Brady walked up behind her and put his arms around her waist, resting his chin on her shoulder. "What do you think about your first Jubilee snowstorm?"

She tilted her head slightly to look at him and smiled. "I think it's the most fun I've had in a long time."

THE RELENTLESS HOWLING of the wind had become the only constant in Ava's world. She felt like she was about to freeze solid as she huddled inside of her truck. Darkness had descended over the mountain hours ago, the only light the occasional glimpse of the moon through the trees.

Her gas had long ago run out and with it, the last

bit of warmth that she had. Her eyes were heavy, like big pieces of ice, with exhaustion and defeat. They kept fluttering closed, and she could feel her consciousness teetering on the edge.

There was a part of her that just wanted to close her eyes and go to sleep. It would be a peaceful death, she supposed. But it was then, just in that little bit of awareness that she still had, that she saw the distant glow of something piercing through the white expanse around her. A bright reflection in her side mirrors.

She blinked several times, disbelief mingling with a flicker of hope. "Oh my gosh, is this it?" she said to herself. "Is that the light that I'm supposed to go toward? Do I have to get out of the truck to actually go toward the light? I don't see my grandparents... Where are the angels?"

She just kept whispering these things to herself, half expecting an answer to come and half hoping for some kind of miracle. The light got brighter and brighter, cutting through the fury of the snowstorm, and then she realized it was right behind her truck. She squinted against the brightness, wondering if she was dreaming or about to go to heaven. She really couldn't figure out what it was.

Before she could think too much more about it,

her truck door swung open, and a figure emerged from the blizzard. This man seemed to look like the very essence of strength and safety. He was tall, had the broadest shoulders she'd ever seen, and was cloaked in a very heavy jacket that did little to conceal his powerful muscular build beneath. His face was framed by a beard that hinted he spent his days in the wilderness. He looked concerned, yet determined.

But it was his eyes that she noticed the most. They were clear blue and steady underneath the brim of his snow dusted hat. They captured her attention, his piercing gaze that seemed to see right through the storm and right through her. All she could compare him to was a modern day lumberjack or some kind of hero carved out of old tales where strength and tenderness could coexist effortlessly.

He said nothing, but reached in for Ava, his large hands gentle but firm as they literally scooped her out of the confines of her frozen truck. The warmth of his grasp enveloped her like an electric blanket, chasing away the chill that had seemingly seeped into her bones. He carried her toward the light, his Jeep she now realized, and she couldn't help but feel as though she had been taken from the jaws of death.

Once she was inside of his vehicle, heat blowing

directly on her, the storm continued to rage outside as he pulled away from her truck, still saying nothing. She noticed the rugged handsomeness of his features, the depth of his gaze as he stared at the road. There was a quiet strength that radiated from this man. Maybe she was dreaming. Maybe she had gone to heaven, because she had certainly never seen a man that looked like this on earth. She was too shaky to say anything as her teeth were still chattering.

This man was like some sort of larger-than-life hero, a beacon of hope in her darkest hour. "Thank you," she finally whispered when she could stop her teeth from clanging against each other. He didn't say anything, but merely nodded as he focused on driving them to safety. She didn't know where he was taking them, but she didn't care at this point. All she knew is that right now she was safe.

CHAPTER 3

*T*he drive away from her vehicle felt surreal to Ava. The more she warmed up, the more she wondered where she was going and whether this man was safe. Obviously, he had saved her from a certain death on the side of a mountain, but she had to wonder if he was some sort of ax murderer or something. Heck, he wouldn't even need an ax. He could break someone in half with a couple of his fingers.

He still remained silent as he navigated the Jeep through the snowstorm. At first, she found it odd that he wasn't speaking, worried that maybe he was some sort of lunatic, but she herself could not navigate such a snowstorm. Her mind raced with some dark thoughts, her imagination conjuring the worst scenarios, like maybe he was taking her to some remote cabin to kill her. But then she thought, why would he go to so much trouble to go out in a snowstorm looking for somebody to take back to his cabin to kill? That didn't make much sense. Maybe the exhaustion and the fear had worn her down.

The Jeep finally turned down a road and then slowed to a stop. When the door opened, the biting cold rushed in again, snapping her back into the present moment. He got out, came around to her door, opened it gently, and then offered her his hand, an unspoken request. Her survival instinct urged her to take it because she didn't really have any other options. Asking him if she could just sit out in his Jeep with the heat on all night probably wasn't going to work. She got out, and they approached a cabin. The windows were aglow with a warm light pushing back against the complete darkness in the surrounding woods.

He opened the door, and they stepped inside as Ava braced herself for whatever she had convinced herself was coming. But even though she was a bit scared of this man, she couldn't help but feel a warmth envelop her as she walked into the cabin. He finally spoke for the first time since finding her, as he took off his coat and hung it on a hook by the door.

"You'll be safe here," he said, as he moved over to stoke the fire. She watched him, her fear battling with the incongruity of the situation.

So far, this man that looked like he could kill her with one move of his hand was showing her nothing but care and kindness. He prepared a place for her to rest on the sofa with a blanket and a pillow. She looked at all the details of his small cabin. A bookshelf full of books. A few photographs of smiling people on the mantle. A pot of what seemed to be soup simmering on the stove. This didn't look like a predator's den, but signs that she was in the house with somebody who seemed quite normal.

He caught her looking at him, "My home," he said. "You needed help. You're safe here, I promise."

She wanted to believe him and let go of the fear that had clenched her heart since she first drove up the mountain. The logical part of her mind started to see the situation for what it was. It was a rescue, not an abduction, but the emotional toll of the past few hours, and really the past few days, made her wary about everything. She nodded and then sat down on the sofa by the fire, wrapping herself in the blanket.

She watched him move around the cabin, the

light casting shadows that softened his features. She tried not to stare at him, but it was hard. He was very good-looking. Probably the best looking man she'd ever seen in her life, which was why she thought he was some sort of hallucination before her impending death. For the first time since she had gotten stalled in the snow, she felt a little bit of hope even though she didn't know where her dog was or where she was going to end up. Maybe she was at least wrong about this man, and maybe he would be able to help her turn things around.

JACK WAS TRYING NOT to look at the woman he had just rescued. Anytime there was a snowstorm on the mountain, he felt it was his responsibility as one of the only people who lived on the mountain to go out in his Jeep and make sure nobody was stranded on the side of the road. He had waited several hours before doing it, honestly trying to talk himself out of it. It was cold, obviously, and he had a pot of soup cooking. What in the world did he need to get in his Jeep for and go out and try to be a hero? There probably wasn't even anybody stuck on the mountain. But for some reason, the feeling kept nagging at him, so he had gotten in his Jeep, determined to drive up and down the mountain one time and then get back home and enjoy his evening. As soon as he had seen her truck, he'd known he had to do something.

Having a Jeep, he was involved in different groups all over the mountain areas that helped rescue stranded drivers in situations just like this. Usually he was towing somebody, but this was too far gone. When he pulled up and saw her sitting there and then looked in the window and saw that she looked like she was falling asleep, he knew she had been there way too long. There was no time to tow her vehicle or even have a conversation. All he knew was that he needed to rescue her. When they had been walking to the cabin door, he let himself take a quick glance at her.

After having seen her when he picked her up out of the truck, he knew she was about his age and a very beautiful woman. That was something he was trying not to think about. What did it matter? Maybe she was married. Maybe she was engaged. Maybe she wasn't interested in a big giant that lived out in the woods and had a bushy beard. But he couldn't help as he saw her walking to the door, the snowflakes melting in her thick, long red hair that cascaded down her back like a fiery waterfall.

He glanced and saw her blue eyes, which were wide and reflected a mix of fear, probably of him more than the storm at that point, and relief. He was immediately struck by her beauty and it reminded him of a long-standing resolution that he was going to steer clear of getting too involved with any women or trying to play the hero. It was a pattern. That's what a therapist had said years ago when he had bothered to go talk to somebody about it.

These days, he decided that maybe he was just going to be a mountain man who lived out in the wilderness and occasionally came out to rescue stranded drivers. It was a life, maybe not a great one, but it was something. He had always been drawn to rescuing those in need, and many times he found himself lost along the way. Nobody ever bothered to try to rescue him. He tried not to think about it. But here he was again, rescuing someone that he didn't even know. This time, it felt different. He had never brought anyone home from the side of the mountain. He usually just pulled them out of the snow so they could make their way to the city, but this storm was way too bad. There was no way pulling her out was going to do any good right now.

He got her situated on the sofa and then brought her a small bowl of hot soup. She seemed to be starting to warm up as she shed the blanket and just sat on the sofa quietly eating.

"I'm Jack Sullivan," he finally said, trying to keep his voice steady. Silence had enveloped the room. He knew he had made it awkward by looking at her. He just couldn't stop thinking about how beautiful she was.

He tried to keep his introduction brief. His nature was not to divulge more than was necessary, especially to somebody he had just met.

"I used to be a deputy here. Now I work in private security, and I'm with a Jeep group that goes out and rescues stranded drivers in situations like this."

She nodded. "I'm Ava. And thank you, Jack, for everything."

The air between them seemed charged. Jack was aware of his own rising interest in her and consciously steered his thoughts back to something more immediate.

"My dog," she suddenly blurted out before he could say anything. "She ran off when my truck got stuck, and I have to find her."

He looked at her for a moment. "We'll start looking at first light," he promised. "The storm's too strong right now. It's not safe." He watched as she processed the words he was saying. Her initial panic seemed to relent just a bit. He understood that kind of bond to a pet. His dog had only recently passed away, and he was missing that companionship out in the woods. Here he was having reservations about getting too involved, but now committing to some sort of search party for her lost dog. "We'll find her. What kind of dog is she?"

"She's a boxer," Ava said.

He nodded. "Boxers are strong dogs. I bet she'll be fine." He hoped he was right, and he hoped that promising to find her was something he could actually do, not just for Ava's sake, but to prove to himself that he could help someone without losing himself in the process.

She seemed to take comfort in that assurance, saying a soft thank you. As she finally seemed to relax a bit onto the sofa, he walked over and busied himself with stoking the fire, trying not to look at her, trying not to touch her beautiful hair.

The cabin warmed up even more, and he found himself stealing glances at her. He picked up a book and tried to read it, but all he did was keep looking over the pages at her beautiful, simple profile. He settled into the chair, and she continued eating her soup. He couldn't shake the feeling that this rescue might be different than all the others. Somehow this woman had already breached his defenses. The storm raged outside, but Jack was facing one of his own. The battle between his instinct to protect himself and keep detached, and making a connection with the woman sitting just across from him.

CLEMMY DECIDED it was finally time to close the bookstore for the night. She had stayed open a little later than she had anticipated when a couple of regular customers came in looking for books to keep them busy during the snowstorm. As she stepped out onto the sidewalk wearing her hefty winter boots and her thick coat, she turned the key in the lock, hearing the gentle echo of the sound across the town square that was covered in snow.

She stood there for a moment looking around to see if there was anybody else as crazy as she was to be out in this mess. There was nobody. Thankfully, she had a vehicle with snow tires, and she knew that she could make it to her house pretty easily, but she wanted to make it home in a hurry before it got any thicker out there. She adjusted her scarf and pulled it tight around her neck and started walking down the sidewalk toward her vehicle.

The snow crunched under her boots, and it was all that she could hear on this quiet evening. She couldn't shake the feeling of unease knowing that there were probably people out there struggling in the cold. Maybe they had lost their heat, maybe their car had broken down. There was so much that could and would happen in Jubilee during these kinds of snow events.

There were always people to help, and she hoped that everybody was safe. At morning light, she would drive back to her store and try to help anybody that she saw along the way. She would also call friends from church and other friends in her circle to make sure that everybody was okay.

Just as she reached her car, which was only parked a short distance from the bookstore, a sudden movement caught her eye. Startled, she turned just in time to see a boxer dog, its coat dusted with snow, running down the sidewalk at full speed toward her.

Clemmy barely had time to react before the dog leaped in the air, its momentum carrying it straight into the open door of her car. She had opened the passenger door, put in her tote bag, but didn't even get the chance to close it before the dog was sitting in the seat, panting and wagging its tail frantically.

Where had this dog come from? She'd never seen it before. In the mountains it was pretty common for dogs to run free, something that really frustrated her at times, but she hadn't seen this dog. It was obviously a purebred, and it seemed very well cared for.

"Whoa there," she said, both surprised and amused. She looked at the tag on the dog's collar, but didn't see any name or phone number. The dog was panting heavily and didn't seem interested at all in getting out of the car, not that she would've asked it to. It was looking at her like it was asking her for help, but she couldn't figure out what kind of help it needed.

"Well, you're a friendly one, aren't you?" she said, as she patted the dog's head. The boxer wagged its tail crazily in response, its tongue lulling out. She figured it was probably cold, hungry, and needed water. She looked again at the little tag and saw the name Millie. That was all it said, no phone number.

Clemmy looked behind her. The street was still empty. Nobody was running after a dog. After all, who would be out in this snow walking their dog, anyway? She knew she couldn't leave it out in the cold, not with the heavy storm continuing to get worse.

"It looks like you're coming home with me then," she said. It wasn't the first time she had taken in a stray, though none of them had ever entered her world with such enthusiasm.

She closed the car door and walked to the other side, sliding in behind the steering wheel. The dog laid down like she was so thankful to be somewhere safe. She wondered what her story was, where had she come from. She started the car and turned on the heater, glancing over at the dog, who was now comfortably sprawled on her passenger seat.

"I guess we'll have to figure out where you belong in the morning," she said, half expecting the dog to respond to her. They drove home in the quiet, just the car radio breaking the silence. Millie seemed to be grateful as she settled into a long sleep on the drive home. Clemmy felt a warmth that had nothing to do with the heater. She had missed having a sense of companionship. Maybe she should get her own dog, but right now she was worried about this one.

AVA HAD NEVER FELT SO awkward. As she sat wrapped in a blanket near the fire, the chill finally falling out of her bones, she watched Jack reading a book in the chair. This was by far the weirdest night she'd ever had. First, she had gotten stuck in a snowstorm and run off the road. Then she had lost her dog. Then she had been right at the verge of death when a giant lumberjack rescued her and took her to his cabin in the woods. This was a story that nobody was going to believe.

Now, she was sitting on his sofa having finished a wonderful bowl of soup while he read a book like nothing was going on. She didn't know what to make of any of it. All he seemed to care about was making sure that she was comfortable, and he had promised that he would help her find her dog. But right now, she didn't exactly know what to make of the entire situation.

Finally, he closed his book and looked at her with inquisitive eyes. She could tell that he had worked as a deputy, maybe some kind of investigator that questioned people under one of those harsh lights in a small room at the police station.

"So Ava," he began, "what brings you out to Jubilee, especially in the middle of a storm like this?"

She felt a knot tighten in her chest. She couldn't

possibly tell him the truth. There was no way she was going to tell him that she was a runaway bride, fleeing from a life that felt more like a gilded cage, and that her fiance was a man who was famous, and that she had somehow put herself in the middle of a reality show. That story was one she wasn't going to share. After all, she wanted this man to respect her enough to help her find her dog and be on her way as soon as possible. Obviously, he didn't watch reality TV or he would've immediately known who she was. There weren't many women with bright red hair and clear blue eyes on reality TV shows where they competed to marry a man. She was embarrassed to even think about it. How exactly would that go?

"Well, hunky lumberjack, I was desperate to get married, so when a reality TV show came up where I could compete to marry a wealthy man, I signed up like an idiot. Turns out, the man picked me, but I don't love him. He's kind of a tool, to be honest. So, on our wedding day yesterday, I climbed out of the bathroom window like something out of a romcom movie and managed to almost get myself killed and lose my dog."

She drew in a breath, her mind racing to come up with a story that would explain her presence without telling too much, "I'm a writer," she lied, the words tumbling out of her mouth. "I've been feeling a little stuck lately, creatively, and I heard about Jubilee. I saw a YouTube video, and it showed how it was a place of natural beauty and quiet inspiration. So, I just thought the change of scenery might help a little bit. So, I rented a car and drove up here hoping to find a cabin where I could work."

None of it really made any sense. First of all, she hadn't rented a car. She was driving an old red truck that her father had left when he passed away. She had helped her grandfather restore it over the years, and when she had become an adult, he gave it to her. It was a rickety old thing. People laughed at her when she drove up in it, but she just couldn't seem to let it go. It was probably one of the reasons why it broke down so easily as old as it was. But still, she had told the lie, so she had to pretend that it was a rental truck. Jack wasn't buying it.

"You rented an old vintage truck to drive over a mountain in a snowstorm?" He looked at her, his eyes squinting.

"I know it doesn't make a whole lot of sense. You see, there's this place in the town where I live where you can rent old vintage trucks, and I just thought it would be so cute to drive up to the mountains and take pictures with it."

She hoped he was buying this, but she was pretty sure he wasn't. Still, he nodded his head slowly, eyed her carefully, and leaned back in his chair.

"Makes sense," he said. "Jubilee has a way of bringing out the best in people, giving them space to create and think. But you sure picked one hell of a time to come looking for your inspiration."

"Yeah, I didn't really check the weather. That was a mistake on my part, obviously."

"Obviously," he agreed.

She smiled sheepishly, trying to play along with her own lie. "I just didn't expect this storm. My timing could have been a lot better, but either way, here I am. And I'm sorry to have interrupted your night."

"Like I said, I go out and try to help people when I can. No problem. There was plenty of soup."

They sat there quietly for a moment, a tension hanging between them. "Well, you're safe here for now," he reassured her. "Once that storm clears, I'll help you get to town. We'll look for your dog, and then you can be on your way."

She nodded, grateful that he understood and that he was offering to help. Now, she just had to pretend that she was a writer. The one thing that she wasn't very good at was writing, so she hoped he didn't ask for a sample. In reality, she was a hair stylist, but she wasn't going to offer to cut his hair or give his beard a trim.

They continued to chat here and there as he picked up his book again. The storm outside whirling and howling was a constant backdrop to their conversation. All that she could think about was that her dog was out there somewhere, and she hoped that Millie could somehow survive until she could find her. Morning couldn't come soon enough.

CHAPTER 4

*A*s the storm raged outside Madeline's cozy cabin, there was a warmth formed by the friends and family gathered inside. Madeline had found a game on her shelf called Truths Unveiled, and it had cards that you would answer questions about. Everybody agreed it would be a fun game to play and get to know each other better.

"Okay," Brady began. "This card asks, what's a dream you've never told anyone?" He paused for a moment as everybody in the room looked at him. "Well, I've always wanted to do something, and I think it's pretty silly, but I'd like to learn to paint. I spend so much time working with my hands on the farm, getting them dirty in the soil, taking care of the animals, that it seems like it would be pretty cool to create something beautiful on a blank canvas."

Madeline smiled. "Brady, I think that's great. You really should pursue it. I know they have some art classes in town."

He shrugged his shoulders and nodded. "Maybe, one day."

Jasmine drew the next card. "Describe a moment where you felt truly brave," she read aloud, her voice steady. "Well, for me, it was the day I decided to leave my ex. It took every ounce of courage I had to grab my daughter and take off, but I knew it was the best thing for both of us. And now, living this life shows me that I made the right decision." The room fell silent, the weight of her words hanging in the air like a thick fog.

Madeline reached over and squeezed her hand. "Your strength is inspiring, Jasmine. You and little Anna here are incredibly brave."

Anna drew her own card. "If you could change one thing about the world, what would it be?" She sat there and thought for a moment, looking at the ceiling as she tapped a finger on her chin. "Well, I think I would make it so that everybody has a safe place to call home and a great family where they feel loved and protected, because I think everybody deserves that."

Jasmine reached over and hugged her daughter. "You're a sweet little girl, my Anna Banana," she said.

Eloise drew the next card and shared a lighter story from Madeline's childhood that got everyone to laugh. The game continued, each person sharing little pieces of themselves, having conversations and enjoying the time together. Connecting with others on a deeper level was something that people often missed, but Madeline was grateful to have these people who were willing to have conversations and tell the truth about their hopes, fears and dreams.

When they placed the last card back in the box, the storm outside seemed to let up just a little bit so that they could see the moon again, reflecting off the mountains beyond. She walked over to the window and looked outside, and Brady walked up and put his hands on her shoulders.

"Did you have fun playing the game?" he asked.

She turned around and kissed him softly on the lips. "I always have fun anytime I'm with you."

AVA STOOD up and stared out the window, watching the snow fall down. This seemed to be the longest night of her life. Every moment felt like it was an hour as she worried about Millie being out in the woods. It wasn't so much that she was worried about predators. Every living thing was probably in a den somewhere waiting out the storm, but Millie was not exactly an outdoorsy dog. Most of the time she wore her pink sweater during the winter time, and Ava took her outside on walks. She had special treats, her favorite fluffy bed and a stuffed animal she carried around like a baby. She wasn't exactly the type of dog that was going to do well surviving in the wilderness by herself for very long.

The cabin felt both warm and confining, comforting and cozy. She was acutely aware of her dependence on this man who had saved her that she really didn't know.

Her mind raced with all kinds of plans she was coming up with to try to save Millie and then to save herself. Jack must have sensed her restlessness.

"I know you're worried about your dog," he said, walking up behind her. "We'll start searching as soon as this storm lets up, but for now, you need to get some rest."

She wanted to protest and tell him that she

needed to get outside immediately and call for her dog again, but she knew that was stupid and irresponsible. She wasn't going to put this man in a dangerous situation, and surely if she walked outside to try to search, he was going to follow her. So she nodded, silently acquiescing. She was tired anyway.

"Care for some peach cobbler?" he suddenly asked out of the blue.

"Peach cobbler?" she said, smiling slightly.

"I had some made to eat after dinner. I didn't want to eat in front of you."

She smiled and nodded, "I could eat some peach cobbler."

He made two plates, and they both sat down at the small dining table. She took a bite and wanted to groan, but didn't want him to think she was weird. It was so good. It had been a long time since she'd had home cooked southern meals, and she'd missed it.

"You made this?"

"I did," he said nodding, taking another bite.

"Wow. I don't know many men who can cook like this."

He smiled, "I learned a lot from my grandma. She was a proper southern woman and the best cook I've ever known."

"My grandmother wasn't a great cook. I missed

out on that," she said laughing. "In fact, none of the women in my family were very good cooks."

"What about you?"

"I wouldn't say I'm a great cook, either," she said chuckling "But I try."

"That's all you can do," Jack said.

After they ate, he showed her to a small room off the main living area. "You can sleep here," he said, pointing to a neatly made bed with a pink and blue quilt. "It's not much, but you'll be comfortable."

"Thank you," she said. The reality of spending the night under the same roof with this burly-looking, Hollywood-hunky man and relying on his hospitality was a stark reminder of how quickly her life had just veered right off course. Just a day ago, she was standing in front of cameras with one of the richest men in America getting ready to marry him, and now she found herself in the woods with a muscle man with a bushy beard who made great peach cobbler.

"Get some rest," he said before walking out and closing the door behind him.

Alone in the room, she sat on the edge of the bed, the fabric of the quilt soft under her hands. This man had shown her a lot of kindness, had rescued her from the side of the road and fed her, had given her a safe place to sleep and offered to help her find her dog. She was starting to feel very grateful for the fact that this stranger had come to her aid.

She laid back against the bed and stared at the ceiling, which was made out of wood planks. She realized that for the first time since she had fled her wedding, she felt safe. The storm might rage outside, and she was worried about Millie, but for tonight, she was warm, fed and sheltered. She closed her eyes, trying to push aside her worries, focusing on the kindness that she had encountered on the worst day of her life, and the stranger who had shown her unexpected care. She found a momentary peace, and before she knew it, she was fast asleep.

AVA OPENED HER EYES, noticing light coming through the curtains. The snow was still falling against the windowpane, but the storm seemed to have settled a lot. Although the snowflakes still looked large as they fell from the sky, the wind had let up.

She slowly stood up and rubbed her eyes. Walking over to the window and looking out, what she saw looked like a winter wonderland from a movie. She had to admit it was beautiful out there in the forest. She didn't know how far off the road she was at his cabin, but she had never seen so much snow in her life. She knew the search for Millie was going to be difficult, if not dangerous, even though the wind had died down. She felt panic fluttering a bit in her chest. She thought this morning she would wake up, see some melted snow, and be able to go out and look for her loyal companion. But now she didn't know. The thought of her dog out there suffering because of Ava's own actions made her feel awful. It was unbearable.

She walked out into the living room and saw Jack stoking the fire. He must have noticed her distress the moment she stepped out of the room as he handed her a mug of steaming coffee.

"Hey," his voice was soft, a grounding presence in her panic. "I know you're worried. We'll start looking for your dog as soon as it's safe. I promise. I didn't know if you took cream and sugar."

She looked at him. "This is fine. Thank you." Normally she did take cream and sugar, but she didn't want to put this man out anymore than she had to.

"It's still pretty thick out there, although I'm hoping this snow will let up at some point today. I was going to turn on the weather in a moment and take a look."

"Thank you. I appreciate it. And again, I'm sorry that I've been such an imposition. All of this is my fault for trying to drive over a mountain in an old truck without looking at the weather. I guess I wasn't thinking clearly."

"Well, we all do that at times. And you're not imposing at all. I'm always here alone, and it's nice to have some company. We'll find your dog. I'm sure of it."

"But there's so much snow," she said, trying to swallow the lump in her throat and not burst into tears at the thought of her dog being stuck out in that. He set his mug down on the table.

"This isn't the first storm I've weathered, and it won't be the last. I got to you, and it was much worse outside than it is now. Snow makes things harder, but not impossible. We'll find her, okay?"

She searched his eyes wanting to believe him. He had such confidence, such bravery. It touched something deep within her. She wasn't sure if she'd ever met anyone with such a deep sense of compassion.

"Thank you," she whispered, feeling the coil of panic that had tightened itself around her begin to loosen. "I can't lose her. She's all I have."

He nodded. "You won't lose her. I'm here and we're in this together now. I should be able to get your truck towed back here today, at least. I'll call one of my Jeep buddies, and he'll bring it over. I'll fill it up with gas I've got left over from using my mower last summer."

She didn't know why this guy was helping her like he was. He didn't know her from anywhere. She watched him prepare for the day, his movements deliberate and focused as he stoked the fire and started breakfast. The snow continued to fall, so beautiful and peaceful, yet causing her so much turmoil. Though they were trapped by the snow, she felt safe, and she was glad to have a companion that could take care of her. It had been a long time since she had felt anything like that.

DANG IT. She was even more beautiful in the morning light. Jack moved around the cabin, trying to distract himself from the beautiful redhead sitting on his sofa by the fire. This was like something out of a movie or one of those romance novels his grandmother used to read. He checked the windows for drafts, made sure they had enough firewood to last through the day, and started breakfast - scrambled eggs, bacon, homemade biscuits. It was the thing he made most mornings, even when he was by himself.

This woman had become his unexpected guest, but he found himself hoping she never left. She had a rare beauty he could stare at forever... and possibly get locked up on stalking charges.

Maybe he just hadn't been around a woman for so long. He'd been a deputy for many years and developed an intuition when somebody was running, when somebody was hiding, and Ava was no exception. She'd arrived in the middle of a storm in a rickety old vintage truck that had broken down on the mountain.

That didn't make any sense. Why would anybody be running so fast in such a vehicle without even paying attention to what the weather was going to do? But still, she was a stranger. She wasn't under arrest. As far as he knew, she hadn't broken any laws. It wasn't like he could force her to answer questions.

He slyly watched her from across the room, trying to appear as if he was absorbed in whatever he was doing at the moment, which was way more than he normally did on a daily basis. He just needed to focus on something. As he let the eggs cook for a moment, he walked over and topped off her coffee. He watched how she looked out the window frequently, probably hoping that her dog would just be standing there. It made his stomach clench that she was so worried.

He knew better than to pry. People had reasons for keeping secrets, and he respected it. He had secrets of his own, but he had spent his life protecting other people, ensuring their safety, and he had this protective urge towards Ava that he had never felt before. It wasn't just the fact that he had been a deputy that made him feel that way. There was something more, something about her inherent strength, and yet her vulnerability that spoke to him in a way that felt very worrisome at this point.

He wondered what she had left behind. What had driven her to flee into a snowstorm? Fear? Desperation? Was somebody trying to hurt her? Jack understood the weight of decisions and how they could cast shadows on the present. He'd seen it in the eyes of many individuals he had encountered in his line of duty. He could tell that she wanted to start new, that she was trying to get away with the only thing she had left, as she put it, her dog. He was determined to make sure that she got that dog back in her arms as quickly as possible.

He turned off the stove and walked over to the fire, adding another log, making a silent promise to himself that he would provide her with a sanctuary, help her find her dog, and get her on her way. It would be the best thing for both of them.

MADELINE DROVE her golf cart down to Brady's farm. She was so excited to get to see his new home, which had now been completed. He had kept her out of it so far, wanting to surprise her with what he had designed. He had pretty much done everything himself, from the drawings to a lot of the work. Some of his friends had come over to help, as well as a few contractors who needed to do some things, like electrical and plumbing. It truly had been a labor of love for Brady to build this house that he, his sister and his niece would live in. The crisp morning air nipped at their cheeks as Brady led Madeline across the snow-dusted ground toward his new home. It was a rustic log home, much like hers, that stood proudly at the edge of his small farm, over-looking the land and a small pond.

"Well, here it is," Brady said, pointing to it, a smile on his face. She knew he had to be so proud of his hard work. "This is a new start for Jasmine, Anna and me."

He held Madeline's hand as he opened the front door, and they walked inside. It truly took her breath away. The scent of the rich wood filled the air, giving her a sense of warmth and comfort like she felt at her own cabin. The inside was very spacious, but cozy, with exposed beams and tons of natural light streaming through the large windows that gave a panoramic view of the forest beyond the farm. She could even see some of the mountains off in the distance. Brady also had a wood stove that sat in the corner of the open living room.

"This will keep us plenty warm through the winters," he said, his hand resting on the cast iron. "It took us a while to get it installed, but it's exactly what this place needed."

"It's beautiful, Brady. I love these beams going across the ceiling. It gives it so much character."

"Come on. Let's take a look at the kitchen," he said, pulling her hand. It was practical and well-appointed with sturdy, solid wood cabinets and modern appliances. She knew many meals and conversations would be shared here. There was a large handmade dining table right next to the kitchen.

"Is this Amish?" she asked.

"Yes, it is. You can't hardly move this thing. It took me and three of my friends," he said, laughing.

"Well, it certainly adds to the charm. I absolutely love it. I might have to have one made for my house," she said, winking.

They continued moving through the cabin as Brady showed Madeline each of the bedrooms. Jasmine's room had a small desk by the window where Brady thought she might do some work for Madeline, or read books.

As Madeline's assistant, Jasmine had an office space at Madeline's cabin, of course, but this would be a great way for her to work from home more. She also had her own bathroom, which Brady knew she was going to enjoy after sharing one with him and Anna for months.

Anna's room was much brighter with a view of the pond. It had a space for her art supplies and lots of shelves for her books.

"I wanted to make sure she had her own little place to create and dream," Brady said. He adored Anna. She had been a blessing he hadn't expected.

Brady's own bedroom was all wood from floor to vaulted ceiling, and it had a small deck off of it where he could see a view of the forest beyond. He also had his own bathroom with a beautiful jetted tub and large tiled shower.

Brady took Madeline up into the attic, which was a set of stairs at the end of the hallway. It was a great space for something, although he wasn't sure what, but he had gone ahead and finished it. It had a cute little dormer window that looked out over the woods. When they went back downstairs, they walked outside to look around the exterior.

Brady showed Madeline his plans for another small vegetable garden and maybe even a greenhouse. There was a beautiful covered back porch where Brady had already put a wooden swing. He and Madeline sat down on it and looked out over the forest beyond.

"You know, this is more than just a house to me," Brady said, looking at the land that had been in his family for generations. "This is a chance for us to really put down roots where we can build something that lasts beyond me, Jasmine and even Anna."

Madeline nodded. "It's a beautiful home, Brady. You've done a great job here."

"Mind if I ask you something?" Brady said.

"Of course. What?"

"Will you help me decorate this place?" he asked, laughing.

AVA WAS restless and having a hard time sleeping. She had gone to bed a couple of hours ago, but she kept waking up over and over. Sometimes she was too hot. Sometimes she was too cold. So she decided to get up to go to the kitchen for a glass of water. The quiet of the cabin at night had a calming effect on her. She walked over and picked up a glass beside the sink, filling it up, but then a soft melody drifted through the stillness of the cabin, stopping her in her tracks. It was a guitar playing a gentle, haunting tune that seemed to speak directly to her soul. Suddenly, she heard a voice low and rich, filled with emotion. It was Jack. She had known Jack to be many things so far - kind, strong, a little bit mysterious, protective. She had no idea he could play the guitar, much less sing. It added yet another layer to him that she hadn't imagined.

This man was one of the most surprising people she'd ever met. Drawn to the music, she couldn't help but move quietly down the hallway, her heart seeming to beat in rhythm with the song. The melody guided her to his door, which was slightly open, where she stood listening. The song sounded like something he had written himself, his voice carrying a vulnerability that she hadn't witnessed before in him. It was a beautiful song, talking about the mountains and growing up there.

Lost in the music and the moment, she didn't even register her own movement as she swayed back and forth, and the floorboard beneath her feet betrayed her with a loud creak. The music stopped suddenly, replaced by a very heavy silence. And then moments later, the door swung open. Jack was standing there in the soft glow of lamplight in his room, shirtless, wearing only a pair of sweatpants.

Dear Lord in heaven. Who had muscles like *that*?

His guitar was hanging loosely from one hand. He stood there staring at her, and she couldn't tell if he was embarrassed or curious as to why she was there. She traced the lines of his chest with her eyes, looking at the muscles she hadn't realized were so defined under his heavy clothes. The air between them crackled with a tension that was new and electrifying, and she couldn't seem to stop staring.

"I couldn't sleep. Came to get water and heard music," she stammered like she'd just learned how to talk, her voice barely above a whisper. Her eyes were still looking up and down his torso area, which she knew was completely inappropriate and was super embarrassing when she finally caught his eyes looking at her. He smiled slightly, still holding the guitar.

"I don't usually play for an audience."

"You're really good. You should play for audiences," she said, trying to keep her voice from shaking. Did God really make men that looked like this? He looked like he could push a tractor trailer up the mountain with one hand tied behind his back.

"Thanks. Maybe you'll let me play for you another time when I'm fully clothed? And the sun is out?"

Her face felt flush. "Right. I'd like that. Sorry to interrupt you." She turned as quickly as she could toward her room, but she still heard Jack's last words.

"Anytime."

CHAPTER 5

*I*t was yet another morning on the side of a mountain, and Ava was pacing restlessly, her gaze fixed on the windows as she watched the first rays of sunlight struggle through heavy clouds above the forest. The storm had finally stopped, but left behind a world covered in white. The silence of the morning was broken only by the occasional groan of the trees under the weight of the snow. She turned to see Jack watching her, probably sensing the turmoil that was swirling around in her gut.

"I think it's safe enough to go ahead and take my Jeep to start looking for Millie," he said. "The storm has passed, and I know my Jeep can get through these roads. Besides, I think the city has probably already started clearing many of them."

She turned to him, feeling hope welling up within her again. "Really? You think we can?"

He nodded. "I promised we would look for her as soon as it was safe, and it is safe. So, get on some warm clothes and grab whatever you're going to need for the day. We'll cover as much ground as we can."

Ava quickly gathered her oversized coat, gloves, and a hat, all of which she had borrowed from Jack, and then they headed out to the Jeep. Jack quickly ran around the Jeep and looked at the tires and made sure everything looked okay before they headed out. He threw some extra chains in the back in case they ran across any other stranded drivers along the way. They climbed into the Jeep, and Ava felt a mix of anxiety and hope. There was always the possibility that she would never find Millie, that she would never know what happened to her beloved dog, and that would break her heart into a million pieces. Millie had been the only constant in her life, especially in recent weeks and months. She needed a beacon of light to give her the hope that Millie might actually be alive out there. That she might have survived such a terrible snowstorm.

Jack turned the key in the ignition, and it came to life with a reassuring rumble.

"So we're going to start with the area where you got stranded," Jack said. "Millie might've tried to make her way back there to find you."

Ava's stomach churned. The thought of Millie standing on the side of the road by the truck looking for her made her want to cry. She nodded, trying not to well up with tears as they pulled away from the cabin out onto the road. Jack navigated it with confidence like he'd done this drive a million times, and he probably had.

As the Jeep wound its way through the forest and toward the place where she had gotten stranded, Ava crossed her fingers in her lap, hoping that when she got there, Millie would come running from the forest, lick her in the face, and they would be reunited once again.

She needed her sweet doggy to get her through the next phase of her life, whatever that was going to be.

As the Jeep made its way up the winding mountain road, Ava was surprised to see just how furious the snowstorm had actually been. The landscape was dotted with vehicles that had veered off path at some point, their drivers underestimating the storm severity just like Ava had. She hadn't even been able to see these vehicles because of the whiteout when she was on the side of the mountain. Now wrapped tightly in her coat, she watched anxiously from the passenger side as she scanned the dense woods, hoping that she would see any sign of Millie.

Jack was focused on the stranded cars and their occupants, his obvious sense of duty evident in his every move. He pulled the Jeep over near the first stranded vehicle, which was a small sedan that had skidded into a snowbank, much like Ava had done.

"Stay here. This won't take long," he said, his tone reassuring. She didn't know this man at all, really. He was still a stranger to her, although he had been kind. But when he said something, there was such a sense of authority and assuredness in his voice that she took him at his word, trusted him. She'd never felt that from any other man before.

Her dating life had been a collection of men who never made her feel particularly safe. She hadn't been abused or anything like that, but she'd always felt like she was on her own in the end. There was no one there to back her up and defend her if the time came. Jack felt like a man who would back up the woman he loved, even if it meant risking his life in the process.

She watched as he retrieved the tow-rope from the back of the Jeep and approached the stranded car. The grateful driver jumped out. She didn't know how long they had been there, probably not nearly as long as she would've been had she stayed in her truck. Jack efficiently tied the rope to the vehicle and guided it back to the road, which had been cleared by the county. His actions were methodical and confident like he had done this so many times he could do it with his eyes closed. He moved from one stranded vehicle to the next, and Ava's admiration for him grew. He was a man who, without any hesitation, lent his strength to those in need.

She found herself distracted from her own worries for a moment, caught up in these profound acts of kindness that Jack displayed when he didn't have to. He wasn't getting paid for this. There was nothing in it for him. He just did it to be kind to other people. It made her think that maybe she should do the same. When was the last time she had done something kind for someone else without anything in it for her? People should do more of that.

Every time he returned to the Jeep to move on to the next vehicle, Ava would look out into the woods in whatever area they were in, hoping that Millie would be out there. But between those moments where she was staring at the woods, she found herself fixated on Jack, watching him work. She saw more than just a rugged exterior of a man who was obviously strong and very capable; she saw a man with a big heart, maybe bigger than the broad shoulders that she couldn't stop staring at.

They continued on up the mountain, and Ava started to realize that Millie wasn't coming out of the woods. She wasn't anywhere to be found. It made her want to burst into tears, but she was too embarrassed to do that in front of Jack. He was so strong and confident helping other people she couldn't break down like a weakling and burst into tears. So she just watched him and tried to focus on his positivity. He believed they would find Millie somehow, some way, and she just had to hold on to that for a little while longer.

CLEMMY STOOD in her kitchen wearing her thickest white bathrobe and holding a steaming mug of coffee in her hand. She watched as the last snowflakes started falling from the gray sky like a farewell to a storm that had been something to behold.

It was a tranquil scene, but she knew that there were probably people out there without power or stranded on the side of the road. She said a quick prayer for them every time she thought about them. She'd had the same thing happen to her many times living in the mountains - power outages and being broken down on the side of the road. But the great thing about Jubilee was that there was always a good Samaritan somewhere to help. People took care of each other in these mountains, and that was something she was grateful for. It was the reason why she would never ever leave.

At her feet was the boxer dog that she had taken in the night before. She looked up and wagged her tail, her gaze fixed on Clemmy with hopeful anticipation. Clemmy smiled down at the dog.

"All right, let's get you fed," she said. She prepared a simple meal for the dog, placing the bowl of food and some water on the kitchen floor. Obviously, she didn't have dog food available since she didn't own a dog herself, so she had boiled some chicken and white rice. The dog seemed to appreciate it greatly.

She had to admit to herself that she enjoyed the companionship. Clemmy only had one child, a grown son who didn't keep in touch as often as she would like. Their relationship had been a bit of a complicated one at times, and she hoped one day they could repair things, that he would come to Jubilee and spend some time with her. But for now, she found solace in her friends and patrons at the bookstore. This dog was filling a space that she didn't know was open, someone to just be glad to see her in the morning, to love her, to want to snuggle with her on the sofa. It was pretty sad when she thought about it, to be in her sixties and feel so alone, yet surrounded by people. Sometimes there was just a need to be loved by somebody in that special way that everyone desires.

She hadn't dated in a while, and she knew she should get back out there. But it wasn't like the dating scene in Jubilee was exactly hopping with excitement. She was starting to feel a bit old, to feel a bit outdated. Clemmy tried not to think about such things because she maintained a positive attitude, but this morning was a little different as she stared out at the snow and realized just how much this dog was starting to mean to her. She couldn't get too attached because she needed to find her owner.

Millie had obviously been well taken care of, and she was probably missing the person who loved her, but maybe she would get her own dog one day. Maybe she needed a little bit of extra love in her life.

She decided that once they got ready for the day, she would print out some flyers to spread the word about the dog in hopes of finding the owner. She couldn't let this bond form any longer than she needed to.

"Once it's safe, girl, we'll find out where you belong," she said. She continued sipping on her coffee. As Millie finished eating, her tail wagging slowly, a silent gesture of gratitude, she kneeled down, stroking her head gently. "I'm going to take care of you until I find your owner," she said, even though the thought of giving up this companion broke her heart just a little.

JACK MANEUVERED his Jeep along the snow-covered mountain roads, his vehicle's tires crunching over the fallen snow. He had done this hundreds of times in his life, either as a deputy or just as a volunteer. Rescuing people on the side of the road was something he was used to. He didn't even give it a second thought. What he was giving a second thought to was the fact that this beautiful redhead was sitting next to him, wrapped up in one of his favorite thick coats, her gaze fixed out on the passing trees and underbrush, looking for any sign of her beloved dog.

Hours had passed since they had started their search, and the sun was climbing higher in the sky with no trace of Millie anywhere. He'd promised that he would find her, and he was starting to regret that promise. What if something had happened to the dog? Maybe he was wrong about the fact that she was still alive.

He was a former deputy and used to tracking people and managing search operations, so he understood the odds and the challenges that they faced. The snow would have erased any tracks Millie might have left. He watched Ava out of the corner of his eyes, noticing that her hope was starting to turn to despair with each passing minute.

"We've covered a lot of ground," Jack finally said, breaking the silence that had settled between them for the last few minutes. "If Millie is out there, she is sure doing a good job of staying hidden. But it's more likely that somebody has probably taken her in. People around here look out for each other and their pets."

She looked at him, searching his eyes to see if he was actually telling her the truth. "I hope you're right, but there don't seem to be very many houses around here. Who would have taken her in? It's not like people were driving up and down the mountain during such a terrible snowstorm."

He knew that she was worried about her dog, but he could sense that there was something else weighing on her, some distraction that went beyond her concern for Millie. "Listen, dogs can travel long distances, especially if they're running. There's no telling where Millie ended up. Did she have a tag?"

Ava closed her eyes and leaned her head back against the seat. "She had a tag that had her name on it, but it didn't have my phone number." He wanted to ask her why. That was a simple thing to do, but he didn't want to make her feel any worse than she already did. "In case you're wondering," she finally said, "I always meant to get my phone number put on the tag. The machine malfunctioned, and that particular day, I was in a hurry, so I just took the tag. I was always going to go back and get a new one. Now I wish I would have."

He looked at her, trying to reassure her. "Look, it's not your fault. You didn't expect that you were going to get stranded in a snowstorm, and your dog was going to run out into the forest in the Blue Ridge Mountains. Everything is going to be okay, Ava."

"How do you know that?" she asked, looking at him. Gosh, he had a sudden urge to pull her close to his chest and protect her from anything the world could throw at her. Where did that come from?

"I don't know. Call it years of experience. I've seen a lot of things that happened that other people would call miracles."

"And you wouldn't call them miracles?"

"Well, yeah, I suppose I would. But let's just say I've seen a lot of hopeless situations turn out okay. You just have to believe that this one will do the same."

She quietly turned her head and looked back into the woods, and he swore he could see some tears welling in her eyes. There was nothing he liked less than seeing a woman cry. It was the one thing that would get to him every single time, and unfortunately, he had had some women in his life that used that as a manipulation tactic. Ava was certainly not doing that.

"Hey," he said, gently pulling the Jeep to a stop at a scenic overlook. "We'll keep looking for her, okay?

But you've got to take care of yourself too. Worrying isn't going to bring her back any faster."

"I know. It's just hard," she said, facing him with a vulnerability he hadn't seen. It caught him off guard. "It's not just Millie, it's everything. There's a lot going on in my life, and I didn't expect to end up here with a stranger. No offense, of course. It's just all a bit overwhelming."

He understood that Millie's disappearance was probably just one part of a larger turmoil that Ava was grappling with. The pieces would eventually fall into place, but he didn't know exactly what they were.

"You're not alone in this," he found himself saying. "Whatever's got you running, you've got a friend here. We'll figure this out together."

She looked at him with a flicker of surprise and something else, maybe relief, flashing in her eyes. "Thank you, Jack. That means a lot," she said, genuinely smiling.

They resumed their journey back over the mountain, but Jack couldn't shake the feeling that their search for Millie was turning into something much deeper, and that was the kind of thing he tried to stay away from. No matter how gorgeous this woman was, he was going to help her find her dog and get her out of town as quickly as possible. He had decided long ago to live his life alone. It was just a lot easier and a lot less heartbreaking.

As the afternoon light started to fade, Ava noticed Jack hunched over the open hood of her truck, his hands moving with a skilled precision as he worked to fix a few things that had broken when she ran into the snowbank.

She stood a short distance away, leaning against the doorframe of the garage, looking at him with her arms crossed. Something was deeply comforting about watching his hands move so confidently and capably over the parts of the truck that had so much history and meaning to her. It reminded her of her grandfather helping her restore the truck all those years ago.

"You know, that truck's more than just a vehicle to me," Ava said.

Jack paused and turned to look at her, listening. She walked closer.

"My dad started restoring it before he passed away when I was really young. This was his project, his dream. He didn't get to finish it." She swallowed hard, the memories bittersweet and vivid. "After he died, it just sat there in my grandfather's garage, collecting dust. When I was old enough to take more of an interest, my grandfather allowed me to help him restore it."

Jack nodded. "It sounds like it has a lot of sentimental value."

She smiled. "A lot. I guess that's why I wanted to take it with me when I left. Finishing it with my Pops meant I always got to keep a little piece of my dad with me, you know? Like I completed something that was important to him, and then I got to keep something important to me in the process."

"I'll take good care of it. I promise."

"I know you will," she said.

Jack returned to his work. She was struck by how much he seemed to know about trucks. There was an intuitiveness to his movements. He never looked anything up on his phone or in a manual. She supposed living out in the remote area he did, he had to know how to fix things.

"You seem good with your hands," Ava heard herself say. She felt her face flush as she realized how that sounded.

"Pretty good," he said, looking up and smiling. "I

had a great dad and grandpa, and they taught me everything I know."

"Well, I'd better get out of your hair," she said, turning to go back into the cabin.

"No, don't. I enjoy the company."

IT WAS another night of Ava watching Jack cook dinner. She had offered several times to help him, but the kitchen wasn't that big, and he seemed to have great skills in there. He didn't need her. He told her to just sit on the sofa and relax, watch some TV if she wanted, but all she could think about was Millie. Well, that wasn't true. She was also thinking about all the other things that had led her up to taking off in her father's old vintage truck and heading off in search of a new life.

Her mother must be quite worried about her by now. There was a wedding, after all, and she never showed up at the end of the aisle. She knew that she should make some phone calls, set some things straight, but the longer she went without doing that, the more she felt like she really couldn't.

She could hear Jack in the kitchen, a sizzle here, a

steady chop there. It was a comforting sound in the background. This was what she had truly wanted in her life. When she was young, she thought she would just meet a great guy, get married, have some kids, have the whole white picket fence type of life, but somehow she'd gotten off track. She had never found her true soulmate, and that's why she had made the choice that she did. How she ended up being a runaway bride. It was embarrassing, and everyone had seen it. She couldn't imagine what people were saying on social media right now. She knew she was never going to be able to start over anywhere without facing the music. There was just no way around it. But she wasn't ready yet. She couldn't, especially not when she knew her dog was missing. Millie was like her child and there was nothing else that she could focus on until she found her.

"Dinner will be ready in a few minutes," Jack said over his shoulder, there was a rich aroma of stew filling the cabin. Ava was quite hungry after a day of looking for her dog.

"It smells amazing. I never would've thought you were a cook," she said, teasing.

Jack laughed. "Is it because I'm such a giant?"

"I mean, you do look like you could play the part

of a lumberjack in a community play or something," she said, hoping not to offend him.

"Well, maybe there's a lot you don't know about me. Cooking is just one of my hidden talents," he said, setting the plates on the table with a flourish that made Ava giggle.

As they sat down to eat, the small talk finally gave way to a much deeper conversation. She really felt like Jack was becoming a close friend. She wondered if when she left here, would she ever be in touch with him again? He didn't seem much like the texting type, and she doubted that he had a Facebook account. Would this just be a memory in her life, a person she'd never see again, but who would know some of her secrets? Maybe it was safe to tell him something.

After all, who was he going to tell? He had a TV, but he never turned it on, that she could tell.

"So Jubilee has always been home for you?" she asked, genuinely curious about this man that had become an unexpected pillar in her life.

"Yeah, always," he said. "Growing up here, it's a unique experience. The Appalachian way of life can be hard at times. We were pretty poor growing up, but you're part of a community that's like a big family. Everyone here looks out for each other."

He chatted a little bit about different times in his childhood in the woods. He talked about community gatherings that felt like reunions and the sense of belonging that had always anchored him to this place. She listened, wondering what it was like to grow up in such a place where you knew everyone and you never had to be alone. It was a stark contrast to the rootless feeling that she had had in her most recent life.

"It sounds wonderful," she said. "To have that type of connection to a place and its people. It's what I always wanted."

"It is great. Although I probably look like a loner back here, I do have a lot of friends in town. They just know that I prefer this lifestyle out in the woods. What about you? What's your anchor?" It caught Ava off guard, the question. Her mind scrambled for a response.

"I'm not sure I have one," she said. "I've been so focused on, well, running away from my problems, I guess that I never stopped to think about where I really belong."

He nodded, his expression understanding. "Running can exhaust you. It takes a lot out of you. Sometimes, stopping isn't about actually giving up. It's about taking care of yourself and finding a new direction."

"I suppose you're right. I'm just at a place in my life where I'm not really sure where I belong. You're lucky to know where you belong."

They continued talking long after the soup bowls were empty and the night wore on. Jack talked about his time as a deputy, the challenges and rewards of serving this community that he loved so much. He also talked about his transition to working in private security.

Ava found herself opening up a little about her own life, her dreams, her uncertainties that had led her to this moment, but she talked around all of it. She wasn't going to tell him all of her secrets because, for right now, it was nice to have someone who didn't judge her. Didn't call her names on social media. Didn't think she was the world's dumbest woman.

"Jubilee has a way of holding up a mirror. It shows you who you really are underneath all the noise and the chaos in the world, and it's not always an easy thing to face, but it is where real change can begin. A lot of people come here to find who they are, and they realize they're so much more than they thought they were."

"You know, maybe that's what I've been looking for," Ava said. "A place where it can reflect the truth back to me and help me figure out who I am."

They continued chatting, and Ava felt more and more comfortable with Jack, but also with this place. She had never been so vulnerable with anybody, and she had to wonder why she felt this way about a man she barely knew.

CHAPTER 6

*A*va had always enjoyed some time alone in the morning. As she sat here in this unfamiliar place, Jack's cabin, and looked out the frosted windows, she held a cup of coffee in her hands. She was sitting at a small wooden table near one of the picture windows overlooking the forest, which was covered in a blanket of white. She could see pieces of green now, which was a good thing. Even though the snow hadn't completely melted, the storm had at least stopped. It left the forest in a state of suspended animation, silent and watchful, the trees heavy with snow. It was picturesque, and under different circumstances, she would have enjoyed it a lot more. But right now, she was worried about her future and her dog.

She was far from feeling peaceful as she sipped on her coffee and bit into a donut that Jack had given her before he went outside. The knot of worry continued to tighten in her stomach. The plan was to go into town today to continue their search for her beloved Millie and try to figure out a way to move forward. If she couldn't find her, could she even think about leaving town without her dog? How many days would she keep doing this before she gave up hope? She didn't even want to think about it.

It was times like these that she thought about the decisions she had made in the last few months. The decision to marry someone she didn't fully love. The decision to say yes in such a public way. The decision to connect herself to someone so famous that she couldn't get away from the media scrutiny. It was all too much. She didn't know why she hadn't been prepared for it, why she hadn't thought it would be a problem, she didn't even know why she had done what she had done. But all of that was being overshadowed by Jack's quiet kindness and the unexpected sense of safety she had found in his company.

What would happen if he finally realized who she was? The thought sent a shiver down her spine that was unrelated to the cold air outside. She took another sip of her coffee, trying to calm her nerves. She knew that she wasn't going to be able to hide away forever. At some point, she'd have to face the world outside, she'd have to face the judgment and pain. It was all inevitable. She didn't want to drag anyone else into it with her, and certainly not Jack, who had been nothing but nice to her. But on this morning, she would allow herself just a few more moments of solitude while she savored the warmth of her coffee in the quiet of the cabin. She would soon go into town and face the people, none of whom she knew, and whatever recognition might come with that. But until then, she just clung to the calm before the inevitable storm, knowing that no matter what journey lay ahead, she was going to have to face it with as much courage as she could muster.

THERE WAS JUST something about the rhythmic thud of the axe splitting the wood that calmed Jack's inner turmoil. It was crisp outside this morning, the whole forest still filled with snow, and Jack had left Ava inside the cabin to drink coffee and eat something for breakfast before they headed out into town. He stood in a clearing beside the cabin, his breath a thick fog in the cold, while his body moved in a practiced ease borne of the countless winters he had spent out in the forest.

His mind was far from the task at hand, however. He was thinking about the fact that he had a strong inclination to be drawn to people who needed saving, and what it had often done to him in the past. He set another log on the chopping block as his thoughts drifted back to Ava. She was just one in the latest line of individuals he'd found himself wanting to protect, but she seemed different. He couldn't help but feel that way. She wasn't just another random person looking for help. Deep down, he couldn't shake the feeling that he was walking a familiar path, one that might lead him to heartache, just like it had done before.

He remembered Laura, a woman he'd met during his early years as a deputy. She had struggled with an abusive ex, and that had made him want to go above and beyond to ensure that she was safe. He thought they'd had something real, but then found out she was just using him as a shield. She needed help from the danger, and once it passed, she left town without even so much as a goodbye.

That betrayal had really stung. Then there was Sophie, another woman he'd tried to rescue. She had struggled with addiction. He had seen the potential in her and had believed in her when nobody else would, but in the end, his support wasn't even enough. She chose her demons over the life he'd tried to help her build. It was just another harsh lesson in his inability to save someone who didn't want to be saved.

Every time he swung the axe, he grappled with these memories. The woodpile was growing steadily as he thought and thought about how he became entangled with women who saw him as more of a savior than a partner or a best friend. He recognized that this was a cycle he hadn't been able to break on his own, which was why he hadn't dated in several years now.

With Ava, it was something more. There was some kind of connection he couldn't entirely put his finger on, something more than just her needing him. She was hiding from something big, that much was clear, but she seemed resilient. She didn't seem to have an addiction problem. He didn't think an abusive ex was chasing her. She was fighting her own battles and being very secretive about them.

He paused for a moment, resting the axe against

the chopping block. Ava's presence in his world had certainly disrupted the equilibrium of his life, challenging him to consider the possibility that maybe he would get into a new relationship, or maybe he was just being a hopeless romantic. She probably wasn't even thinking about anything like that. They hadn't shared any romantic moments at all. Maybe he was just getting lost in his thoughts and needed to finally start dating again.

After taking a few breaths, he picked up the axe to continue his work. Maybe Ava just represented something in his life, that love was both a risk and a promise. She might not be the woman he ended up with, but maybe he should start pursuing that again. Or maybe he should get some kind of therapy.

As Jack continued pondering his various thoughts, Ava suddenly appeared like a fiery-haired angel in the doorway of the cabin. She was truly stunning. Why wasn't she married to some wealthy man with a giant diamond on her finger?

She was wrapped snugly in one of the blankets from his sofa, framed by the rustic logs surrounding the door. She looked like a picture or maybe a painting waited to be completed. Someone should capture the shot, he thought. She watched him without saying anything, just a slight smile on her face. He kind of liked being watched, especially by a woman like her.

"That looks like a lot of hard work," she finally said, teasing him.

"Not so hard," he said, flexing his muscles and laughing. "How do you think I built these things?"

He swore he saw her blush a bit. "Well, as you can see, I've never swung an axe in my life." She slipped one of her biceps from under the blanket and attempted to flex it. Nothing much happened except that Jack found it incredibly cute.

"Come here," he said without thinking.

"What?"

"I'm going to teach you."

She laughed and shook her head. "No thanks, lumberjack. I'll stay over here where it's safe."

He waved his hand at her. "Come on. Don't be a scaredy cat."

She dropped the blanket and walked toward him, only wearing her long-sleeved shirt and a pair of jeans. "I never back down from a challenge."

Jack wasn't going to let her freeze to death, so he removed his heavy coat and handed it to her. "Here. Take this."

"I'm not taking your coat!"

"Yes, you are," he said, wrapping it around her

and guiding each of her arms into the holes. He could feel her warm breath on his arms, and she smelled like sugar.

"Okay, so how do I do this?" she asked, standing there looking at the stump. The image of her in his giant coat with her beautiful red wavy hair was almost more than he could take.

He picked up a smaller, lighter axe nearby. "We'll start with this one," he said, handing it to her.

She took it and moved it from hand to hand, trying to get a feel for it. He moved closer, guiding her on how to stand and where to aim, his hands moving over hers to adjust the stance. "You want your feet to be shoulder-width apart, get a good grip on the handle, and focus your eyes on what spot you want to hit. Right here should split it nicely," he said, pointing.

This was the first time he'd taught a woman how to swing an axe, and he was having a hard time keeping focused. He was acutely aware of her and the way she moved. The scent of her strawberry shampoo as he leaned in to correct her grip.

He moved, and she stepped back, taking in a deep breath. When she swung, the axe bit into the wood, not quite splitting it but making a measurable dent.

She smiled triumphantly. "That was better than I thought it would be. Can I try again?"

"Of course," he said, crossing his arms and watching her.

Again, she took in a breath, but this time her tiny little frame seemed to grow to twice its size because she swung the axe with way more power than before, splitting the log right down the center. Ava dropped the axe and jumped up and down, like she'd just won the lottery. Without missing a beat, she hugged him tightly, standing up on her tiptoes. Jack thought he might just melt into a large puddle right there on the snowy ground. Before he could put his arms around her, she pulled back and cleared her throat.

"Sorry about that. I might've gotten a little overly excited there," she said, tucking her hair behind her ear. Adorable.

"No problem. That was quite something to watch."

"Well, I'd better go get a shower if we're heading into town. Need to find my Millie girl." She handed him his coat back.

He smiled and nodded. "Right. I'll be waiting."

As he watched her disappear into the cabin,

picking up the blanket on the way, he felt a void. This was no good at all.

As Ava triumphantly returned to her room, she felt a sense of giddiness. Not just at splitting her first piece of wood, but at feeling Jack beside her. The man was like a brick building, tall and strong. She could smell his earthy cologne and feel his warm breath behind her ear. Maybe that's why she'd hugged him. She just wanted to see what it felt like.

She laid out her clothing to wear into town, and then a sense of guilt washed over her. She'd been avoiding something, and she couldn't do that any longer.

She sat on the edge of the bed holding the phone in her hand. Jack was one of those unusual people who still had a landline in his house. He said it was important in the mountain areas because he rarely had a cell phone signal. Right now she was thankful for it.

She dialed the familiar phone number and waited. She thought she might have a full-on panic attack. She had been putting this off and felt terrible about it.

"Hello?" The sound of her mother's voice made her feel warm and fuzzy inside.

"Hey, Mom, it's me," Ava said, her voice cracking.

"Oh my gosh, Ava! Are you okay? Where are you?" her mother asked. She was obviously exhausted from several sleepless nights worrying about her daughter. Ava felt horrible about it, but she had seen no other way. The fact that she was so well-known right now, she worried that her mother would be badgered with questions from people speculating what had happened that day at the wedding.

"I'm okay, Mom. I'm safe," Ava said, rushing to reassure her. "I obviously didn't want to get married. I couldn't go through with it, and I'm so sorry that I didn't call you sooner. I just had a few things happen, and I needed some time to figure things out."

There was a pause for a moment that stretched between them like miles of road. "Oh, Ava," her mother said, sighing. "I've been so worried about you. Everybody has, but you know I didn't want you to marry him. I never wanted you to go on that stupid reality show. I knew that wasn't what your heart wanted or needed. It was a spectacle, and I don't understand why you did it."

Ava's eyes filled with tears. She knew her mother

would accept her no matter what, but she had definitely made a big mistake.

"I know. I guess I just lost myself for a while there, and I'm trying to find my way back."

"Where are you?"

"I don't want to tell you."

"Why? I wouldn't tell anyone."

"I know, but it's just better if you don't know because if somebody comes asking, then you can tell them honestly that you have no idea where I am."

"When are you coming back?"

"Well, that's a problem. I'm not quite sure. I lost Millie."

"What do you mean you lost Millie?"

"Well, I had a minor accident in my vehicle."

"Oh, my gosh! Are you okay? Are you injured? You're not in the hospital, are you?"

Ava chuckled under her breath. Her mom had always been one to jump to the worst-case scenario. "No, I'm fine. I didn't get hurt. I just had a little incident, and when I opened the door to figure out what to do, Millie got out. She ran straight out into the forest, and I haven't been able to find her. I'm not leaving where I am until I can find her."

"I understand, but if you'll just tell me where you are, I'll come to you. Are you alone?"

"I'm not alone."

"What does that mean? Who are you with?"

"Well, this is going to sound crazy, but this really nice man saved me on the side of the road, and I'm at his cabin."

"Oh, my gosh. Ava, are you crazy? He's probably some kind of lunatic. You've got to get out of there. Tell me where you are, or can you call the police as soon as you hang up with me?"

"Mom, calm down. He's very nice. He's harmless."

She sighed on the other end of the phone again. "Ava, you're not making very good decisions. This is just another one of them. You always trust the wrong people."

"You have to trust me, Mom. I know what I'm doing. I know it sounds a little crazy and maybe dangerous on the outside, but I'm safe here. Jack will not hurt me."

"Jack. His name is Jack? Do you want to tell me his last name?"

Ava laughed. "No, I do not. He's a very nice man. He's done a lot of things to help me, and he's going to help me find Millie next. As soon as I have my dog, I'm going to leave. But I can't go without her. You know how much I love Millie."

"I know, dear. I just wish that you would let me

come help you. I can even get some of your friends together to come with me."

"No. I appreciate it, but no. I just wanted to call you so that you would know I was okay so that you would stop worrying."

"Oh, honey, I'm never going to stop worrying. Especially now that I know you're out somewhere with a man you don't know."

"He's been kind to me, more than kind. I feel safer with him than I have felt with anyone in a long time."

"Well, I guess I'm glad to hear that, Ava. I just want to make sure that you're okay. So will you please call me again? Don't let it be so long."

"Of course. And thank you. I promise I'm going to make everything right. You'll see me again very soon, and I'll call you as soon as I find Millie."

"Okay. As long as I know you're safe, that's all I need, but please don't wait too long, okay? I miss you."

"I miss you too, Mom. I'll see you soon. I love you."

"I love you too, Ava. Always."

As Ava hung up the phone, she had a sense of peace, but a tear still rolled down her cheek. That conversation was long overdue. She'd felt terrible about it, keeping her mother in suspense, wondering where she'd gone, but now that she had told her she was okay, she could at least breathe easier knowing that her mom wasn't up all night worried about her. Or maybe she would be, anyway. If she had any idea that the man she was staying with looked like a big, scary lumberjack, she would probably be a little more than concerned.

THE ROADS, finally cleared by the diligent work of some snowplow operators, opened up the world beyond Jack's secluded cabin. Ava felt relieved that they could get out and look for her dog, but also a little trepidation as they drove into Jubilee in the town square. They had a small stack of flyers with Millie's picture printed on them, and she was acutely aware of the risk of venturing into town. She knew that she would possibly be recognized, and that gnawed at her. She needed Jack to continue helping her, and she didn't want him to think less of her when he found out who she was.

But the need to find her dog overshadowed those fears. Jack could tell something was going on. He didn't probe or ask a lot of questions. He had just let her be, which she appreciated. He was like a silent support system sitting beside her and seemed to sense her unease.

"Don't worry, we'll be quick about it," he assured her. Their first stop was at All Tucked Inn, a place that Ava had only heard about in passing from Jack. It was the town's inn, and it was adorable. There was even a little white dog that sat up in the second-story window overlooking the town.

She hadn't planned on interacting with many people in Jubilee, wanting to keep her presence as unobtrusive as possible. As they parked and took the flyers, Ava sucked in a deep breath bracing herself for any unwanted interactions. As they walked into the inn, there was a warmth about it, a stark contrast to the freezing cold air outside. Ava hung back and tried to slightly hide her face as Jack led the way up to the check-in counter. A woman with a kind face and a welcoming smile greeted them.

"Hey, Lanelle. We're hoping to put up some flyers," Jack said. "My friend's dog went missing during the storm."

The older woman, who Ava now knew was named Lanelle, leaned over slightly and smiled at her. "Of course, you can put them up. I sure hope you can find your dog. I'll make sure my daughter,

Heather, knows about it, too. She runs the place with me."

Ava smiled slightly, still turning her head downward. "Thank you. I really appreciate you letting us put up the flyers." Ava was very grateful for Jack referring to it as a friend's dog, keeping her story just vague enough.

He handed a couple of flyers to Lanelle and she promised to spread the word among her guests. A younger man walked in, introduced by Lanelle as Ethan, Heather's boyfriend. Ava was trying to remember all of these names. It wasn't like she was going to ever see these people again, but she thought it was polite to at least know their names.

He had a genuine concern when he heard about Millie. "I'll keep an eye out," he said. "I'm usually all around town during the day, so I'll make sure to mention it to folks. A lot of us are out and about, even in the snow. If she's around, we'll find her."

Honestly, Ava wasn't used to people being so nice to her. The last few months, she had been in a completely different circle of people. These were people who had cared about money and power and fame. Being in this small town was like a culture shock. Everybody was very nice so far. They actually cared that her dog was missing and nobody seemed to care who she was. Still, she was nervous, half expecting somebody to recognize her the moment she had stepped out of the Jeep.

They went back outside to get in the vehicle, and the cold air felt like a slap in the face. "Thank you, Jack," she said as they walked back to the Jeep. "For everything."

He smiled slightly. "We're in this together." For some reason, that gave her butterflies in her stomach. She didn't want to think about why. They continued going around town putting flyers in local shops, and Jack spoke briefly with everybody. He seemed to know every single person in town, which she found very charming, not just for the town, but for Jack.

She was still on high alert with each interaction, but all she was met with was kindness. If these people recognized her, they certainly weren't letting on. She had to wonder if they knew who she was, would she be met with judgment?

As they finished up on one side of the square, she suddenly thought of something. "Hey Jack, do you mind if we run back by the inn? I really need to use the restroom. You can just stay in the Jeep." She hoped he was buying her story.

"Sure, no problem. I'm sure Lanelle will let you use the bathroom."

She stepped out into the brisk air again and walked inside, looking back at Jack one time.

"Oh, hello again," Lanelle said. "Did you need something else?"

"Yes. Actually I was just wondering if you happen to have any rooms available here, even if just for the next night or two?" Lanelle looked at her with an apologetic expression.

"Oh, dear. I'm sorry. We're actually full right now. This snowstorm had everybody seeking shelter, and some are stranded here until the roads leading out of town are more clear."

Ava felt disappointed. "I see. That's all right. Thank you," she said.

It wasn't that she wasn't thankful that Jack was allowing her to stay there, but she felt like an imposition. This man had lived out in the woods for a reason. He liked solitude, quiet, and here she had come barging into his world, not only taking up space in his house, but eating his food and forcing him to look for her dog. She didn't want to do that to him anymore, but there was no place to stay in town except for the inn, and it was full.

And maybe part of it was her attraction to him. I

mean, how many women wouldn't find a tall, handsome, muscular mountain man who played guitar attractive? He was like something out of a romance novel, and she'd had enough romance lately.

She walked back out to the Jeep and got inside, rubbing her hands together.

"Everything okay?" he asked.

"Oh yeah, everything's fine. I just have a really small bladder, I suppose," she said chuckling. Thankfully, he took that excuse and started driving back into town.

AFTER SPENDING some time going around town and putting out flyers, Jack suggested that they head over to the local coffee shop. Perky's was a staple in town and had been run by the same woman aptly named Perky for many years. The coffee was the best in town, and it was such a welcoming atmosphere that Jack felt like Ava would be comfortable there. They also could leave some additional flyers. Perky knew everybody and would be sure to hand them out.

As they went into Perky's, the little bell above the door chimed, announcing their arrival. Several people said hello to Jack as he walked in. It was great to live in a town where you'd been your whole life because people were always so friendly. They knew his whole life history, and he didn't have to worry about being judged. The entire town felt like family to him.

There was the soft murmur of conversations filling the space and, of course, the wonderful scent of coffee filling the air. He noticed that Ava's posture seemed to relax as she saw the charm of the town in the little coffee shop where everybody congregated. It was in moments like these where she seemed to let her guard down a little bit, and he caught glimpses of the person beneath that facade of strength that she wore like armor.

They walked up to the counter, and Jack handed a flyer to the young woman behind the register. He explained the situation and asked her to hang it up on their bulletin board as well as lay a few by the front register. She was happy to do so.

"Can I get you anything?" the woman asked looking at Ava.

"Oh, just a cup of coffee, please."

Jack ordered the same, and then they walked over to a small table nearby to wait. Ava looked around the coffee shop, obviously watching the different patrons read their books, work on their laptops, or just have conversations with friends. Today, it wasn't packed, so it gave her that semblance of anonymity that she seemed to want so much.

The table they chose was near a window that not only overlooked the town square, but the surrounding mountains. "This is just beautiful," she said as she stared out. He took a moment to look at her profile. She had the perfect little button nose, big full lips and the most crystal clear blue eyes he'd ever seen. And of course there was that red hair that had caused his own head to turn the first time he saw her.

Jack kept trying not to think about the night she'd heard him playing guitar. For a moment, he'd been embarrassed. Vulnerable, even. But then he'd seen how she looked at him. Ogled him at one point. It was cute.

Ava's eyes lingered on the view, and she looked like she was a million miles away, yet sitting right across from him. There was a tranquility to her in that moment, but he could tell she was also wrestling with whatever was going on in her life.

He still had no idea what she was running from or the details of her story. She seemed to be shrouded in mystery, but whatever she was getting away from, it was weighing heavily on her. He hated to see it. She seemed like a very nice person, and he always hated when bad things happened to nice people.

"Jubilee is quite the little town, right?" Jack said, trying to start the conversation and maybe offer her a bit of a distraction from whatever was worrying her.

"It is. There's such a charm here. Such a great sense of community. I've never been anywhere like this, to be honest. It's very comforting. Most of the time, I would be very worried about my dog, but for some reason I feel like she's being taken care of and she'll come back to me. I hope I'm right about that."

"I'm sure you are," Jack said smiling at her.

A server brought their coffees over, and they sat there drinking them in companionable silence for a few moments. He wanted to ask her so many questions. Part of him wanted to help, thought that maybe he could do something. Maybe he could solve some of whatever her problem was, but it wasn't his to solve. He barely knew her. He only knew her name, what she looked like and what her dog's name was. He didn't know pretty much anything else, where she'd come from, any of her history. Had she ever had chicken pox? Was she good in school? Had she ever been married? These were things he needed to know to really understand a person. Okay, maybe not the chicken pox. Instead, he decided to just offer her his company, his silent support. It must be scary for a young woman to be out in the world alone, not knowing who she can trust.

She seemed to appreciate his gesture as she would catch his eyes every so often and slightly smile. She had a good smile. Actually, she had a great smile. He had to stop thinking like this. It was almost like he had been watching romance movies when he definitely had not. He just needed to go on a date. That much he was sure of. As soon as he helped this woman get back out of town, he was going to have to find somebody to take out to dinner, at least.

CHAPTER 7

*M*adeline had decided that there was just about nothing better than a night alone with the love of her life. The cabin was quiet, which was a stark contrast to the atmosphere that usually filled it when Jasmine, Anna, and Eloise were around. It seemed like every day was a party. They were always having dinners as a family, and Madeline loved that, but tonight it was just her and Brady. The stillness of the winter evening wrapping around them like a soft, comforting blanket. The snow continued to fall off and on, and it hung in the trees like thick bunches of cotton. Outside, just a tranquil sea of white under the moon's watchful gaze.

A fire was crackling in the fireplace, which

caused a flickering orange light to dance across the wooden walls and ceiling. It created a cozy ambiance that felt magical. Brady had put on some soft music, a playlist that he specifically had picked out for romantic evenings like this. Between the crackling of the fire and the soft music, Madeline felt like she just wanted to curl up in a ball in his lap and go to sleep.

She watched as he moved about the room, adjusting the volume of the music, making sure that it was loud enough for them to hear, but not over-powering. Then he walked over and extended his hand, smiling, that one little dimple popping out and making her heart flutter.

"May I have this dance?" he asked.

Madeline smiled and stood up to face him, putting her arm around his neck as he put his other arm around her waist. They held their hands together, palm to palm, between their chests.

As they began to dance slowly, they blended into each other and almost became one person. She threaded her fingers through the hair at the nape of his neck. Brady didn't keep his hair long, but there was just a little bit there right before he was about to get his next haircut. She liked that little curly area that would sometimes pop out and drive him crazy under his ball cap.

They danced together for what felt like hours, although time always seemed to stand still in their little haven. The world outside didn't matter when it was just Brady and Madeline. She had never felt that way with a man before. All those years of being married and thinking that she was as happy as she could be, she had never known that this was even possible. That these moments that felt like something from a romance novel actually existed for some people. And she would feel eternally grateful that it had happened for her, especially at her age. Her mid-50s wasn't exactly old, but many women she knew either were in unhappy marriages or had not found the right person for them. She would always be grateful that Brady had fallen into her life in such a magical way.

"Thank you for dancing with me," Brady said, his lips pressed close to her neck.

"I wouldn't want to do this with anyone else."

He put both of his arms around her waist and pulled her closer. "It feels like God made you especially for me, Madeline Harper."

She smiled. "I feel the same way. Do you think we'll be together forever? Even when we're old and gray, sitting in creaky rocking chairs on the front porch?"

"No," he said, matter-of-factly. Madeline's heart felt like it stopped.

"No?"

"I would never let your rocking chair be creaky. I'd oil it or buy you a new one."

Madeline slapped him playfully on his chest. "Not funny! You scared me," she said, pressing her cheek to his chest, feeling the thumping of his big, kind heart.

"Seriously, though, I plan to be with you until God calls me home," he said, kissing the top of her head.

She looked up to meet his gaze. "I hated what I had to go through to find you, but I'm so glad I did. There's nowhere else I would rather be," she said, and she truly meant it. There was no place else on earth, not Italy, not France, not Hawaii, not the top of Mount Everest, not the prettiest tropical beach. None of these places could compare to dancing in front of the fireplace with Brady, looking out over the snow-covered Blue Ridge Mountains.

AFTER A DAY of putting out flyers and not finding her dog, Ava should have felt very sad and maybe even a little depressed, but she didn't. Somehow she knew that Millie would be okay and would come back to her in time. Getting to spend the day with Jack had meant more to her than she thought it would. He had been a stranger just a couple of days ago, and in all respects, he really still was. But for some reason she felt close to him, like she could trust him, and she was starting to enjoy these moments. That was dangerous, especially given that she was already engaged to somebody else.

He had decided that they would have chili and cornbread, a recipe handed down from his grandmother and that he said he had made countless times before. Ava watched him move around the kitchen, gathering the ingredients with a familiarity that showed that he had done this many times.

"Can I help you with anything?" she asked.

Once again, Jack looked over his shoulder, a small smile playing on his lips.

"You can just keep me company." Tonight, he seemed to be much more relaxed than he had been when she first met him. He had been all business when he rescued her, which was a good thing because she was at the brink of freezing to death.

But now he had become more comfortable with her around. "Unless you're a cornbread expert hiding your talents," he said laughing.

She shook her head. "I'm afraid my cooking skills are limited, but I am a great conversationalist."

She sat on a bar stool next to the stove while he cooked. The chili was beginning to simmer, filling the cabin with a rich aroma. Jack talked about his grandmother's cast-iron skillet, a family heirloom that had seen decades of meals and memories.

"My grandmother believed that good food can heal just about anything, whether it was because of the food itself or the company that it brought with it. I guess some of that belief stuck with me. Of course, these days I don't get a lot of people coming to visit."

"Why do you think that is? You seem to know everybody in town."

"Well, people are busy. Most people my age have families, children, grandchildren. They have work. I'm just out here in the woods by myself a lot of the time."

"Did you not want a family of your own?"

She realized as soon as she asked it that it was probably none of her business. But she wanted to know how this handsome hunk of a man ended up out in the woods without anyone. She thought at first maybe he was an axe murderer, but he was way too nice for that. She just didn't believe he could ever hurt anyone.

"Of course. I wanted the whole thing, wife, kids, dog. Nothing ever quite worked out the way I had planned."

"So, you've never been married before?" She didn't know why she was continuing to ask these questions that were absolutely none of her business, but she found herself wanting to know more and more about him.

"Never married. I guess that makes me a red flag for a lot of women," he said laughing.

"I don't think so," Ava replied. She wasn't being totally honest. At her age if she had met a man that was never married, she would've thought twice about it, but not with Jack. She took him for a man who had been very serious about his career early on and maybe had missed his chance to meet someone in his younger years.

"What about you? Have you been married?"

Ava wanted to swallow her tongue. How had she not realized that this line of conversation was going to come back to her?

"No, not married yet," she said.

And that was true, she hadn't been married yet.

In fact, on the day that she was supposed to get married, she had fled town, but she didn't need to tell that to him. After all, what would a man think about a woman who had stood another man up at the altar? She decided to try to change the subject.

"Why don't you at least have a dog?"

"Oh, I don't know. I guess I need to look into that. I'm just busy all the time with my different security cases and working here on my land. I don't think it's fair to have a dog if I can't spend a lot of time with him."

"I understand that. They really become like family to us."

"That they do," he said.

She continued watching him move around the kitchen as he got the ingredients for the cornbread. A little while later when it came time to sit down and eat, he served the food by putting it in the middle of the table and putting a white bowl in front of each of them. Ava took her first bite of cornbread.

"Your grandmother knew exactly what she was doing," she said. "This is to die for!"

They chatted about everything and nothing as they ate, mostly about Jubilee and its townspeople, memories that Jack had from when he went to school. Ava didn't have many stories of her own to share. She tried to avoid anything having to do with the last few months or years of her life.

They talked a lot about the cabin and his property and different plans he had for the future, and then together they washed the dishes and put them away. It was such a simple and mundane part of a couple's life, and Ava felt like that's exactly what they were. It was a dangerous spot to be in, finding herself developing emotions for this man when she already had somebody else that she had promised her heart to, although she regretted that now. She didn't know why she had done that in the first place, but she didn't want to hurt Jack's feelings, and she didn't want to just fall for somebody because they had rescued her. Certainly there was some psychological component to all of this. Maybe she needed a therapist.

AFTER THE DISHES were cleared and the leftovers from their meal were put away, Jack stoked the fire. The comfort of the evening had slowly peeled away some layers of reserve between them leaving a space that felt safer to Ava. She watched as the flames danced in the hearth, and she sat down at the end of the sofa with a cup of hot chocolate that Jack had made for her after dinner. She was already stuffed, but she could never say no to hot chocolate with marshmallows on top. He sat down on the other end of the sofa turning slightly.

"I know it's none of my business, but I want you to know that whatever's going on, you don't have to carry it alone. I consider you a friend now. I've shared my grandmother's cornbread with you," he said laughing.

She took in a deep breath. "I know. It's just that I…" she said barely above a whisper.

"It's okay. I shouldn't have asked," he said, waving his hand at her.

"No. I probably should share it with someone."

The problem was Ava didn't think she should share everything. What would this man think about her real story? Maybe she could just tell him a little bit of the truth, but not everything.

"I'm not sure what you're going to think of me if I tell you this."

He smiled slightly. "I've gotten to know you pretty well over the last few days. It's unlikely that anything you tell me is going to change my current opinion of you."

"Hmm, I'm not sure exactly what to think of that,"

she said, smiling slightly. "Okay then." She sucked in a deep breath, willing herself to be brave. What if this man said he wanted her out of his house? That was unlikely, but her anxieties were getting away with her. "I was engaged to someone that I didn't know for very long. Let's just say there was a lot of pressure involved. He's well known. Anyway, our wedding was the morning of the snowstorm."

"Your wedding?" Jack said, his eyes widening a bit. He leaned over and put his mug on the table beside him.

"Anyway, I got up that morning. I went to the church. There was a whole bevy of people there following me around, making sure I was getting ready. And then I went into the bathroom."

"I think I can see where this is going," he said, leaning back a bit.

"I was standing in the bathroom looking in the mirror just about to put on my lipstick when suddenly I realized this was for life and that I was making a really big decision. And I didn't love the man that I was about to go stand with in the church."

"So, what did you do?"

"Well, what I should have done was talked to him, told him the truth. But as I said, there was a lot of extra pressure going on. So…"

"So what?"

"I climbed out the window."

"You climbed out the window?"

"Yeah, and let me tell you that climbing out of a window wearing a full wedding dress isn't easy."

"Wow!"

"And so I haven't talked to anyone since then, except for my mother. I turned off my cell phone for a long time. I didn't want a chance of anybody trying to track me down. I just needed some time to think. And then I ended up on the side of that mountain. Of course, I had to turn my cell phone back on to try to get the signal, but I never did. As soon as you rescued me, I turned it off again."

"What did your mother say?"

"She never wanted me to marry him in the first place, but she's a little concerned that I'm staying at a man's house I barely know."

"I can understand that."

"I told her you'd been very kind to me, but I'm pretty sure she's calling the FBI right about now."

"I don't blame her. I'd be worried, too."

"You don't plan to murder me while I sleep, do you?" she asked, laughing.

"I would never hurt a hair on your head, Ava. And I wouldn't let anyone else hurt you, either."

She cleared her throat. "Thank you."

"So what is your plan? What are you going to do?"

"I have no idea. Right now it's just moment to moment. I need to find my dog. And beyond that, I'm not sure what else I'm going to do. Probably get out of here as quickly as I can, obviously."

"You know, you can't keep running. At some point you're going to have to face the music."

"I know. I'm just not ready to do that yet."

He nodded his head. "Well, like I said, your secret is safe with me, Ava. You found a friend here in Jubilee in a community that looks out for each other. So, trust me when I tell you that you're not alone."

She took a long sip of her hot chocolate and then smiled. "Thank you. You have no idea how much your kindness means to me."

IF THERE WAS one thing that Jack loved about growing up and still living in Jubilee, it was that he had so many friends there. Everybody felt like family and would lend a helping hand anytime it was necessary.

On this cool, crisp morning when there was still

snow dotting the woods, Jack dialed his friend Brady's number. After a few rings, he answered. Brady was always pretty busy running his farm, helping with wildlife rehabilitation, and working as a volunteer firefighter.

"Hey, Brady. It's Jack. Sorry to bother you this morning."

"Oh, no bother," Brady said in his usual cheerful way.

"Listen man, I could use some help today if you've got some time. It's about a dog that's missing, and I've been trying to help someone find her for a few days now."

Brady was always somebody who would lend a helping hand, probably even in times when it wasn't convenient for him.

"Sure thing, Jack. Give me maybe about half an hour, and we can meet at the coffee shop. I'm sure we'll find her."

"Thanks, man. I really appreciate it."

Jack got ready and jumped into his Jeep, heading into town and pulling up outside of Perky's. When he saw Brady's truck, he got out and walked over to him.

"Thanks again for helping me out with this. I really appreciate it. I know you know the area just as well as I do, so I figured having two sets of eyes was better than one."

Brady slapped him on the back. "Yeah, especially when the eyes are as old as yours."

Jack laughed, "I seem to remember that you're older than me."

"Well, let's not talk about that," Brady said. "Wanna take your vehicle then?"

Jack nodded, and they both walked over and got into his Jeep. As they drove along, they chatted about this and that, finally getting to an area where Jack had not searched yet.

"So, who's this Millie belong to? You haven't mentioned it," Brady asked.

"Well, it's just a woman that I helped who was stranded on the side of the road during a snow-storm. She lost her dog when she opened the door to try to get some cell signal."

Brady eyed him carefully. "Sounds like there might be more to this story. Where is this mystery woman?"

"She's at my cabin," Jack said under his breath.

"Wait, a minute. So you picked up a woman on the side of the mountain during a snowstorm, and she's been staying with you at your cabin?"

"Yes, but there's nothing going on. You know I'm

not dating right now," Jack said grumbling. "I just wanted to help her. She's passing through town, going through some stuff. The last thing she needs is to lose her best friend, too."

"I get that, but just make sure you're not getting in too deep," Brady said. "I don't want you getting your heart broken."

Jack looked at him and batted his eyelashes. "Oh, sweetheart. I'm never going to get my heart broken," he said jokingly.

"Seriously, you have a tendency to save these un-savable women."

"Yeah, well, Ava's not that way. She's strong and independent. If you knew her story, you'd understand."

"And you know her story?"

He paused for a moment. "Some of it. I think there might be more. My gut is telling me there is."

"That's the deputy talking," Brady said with a laugh.

"She is running from something. I don't know what it is. Trying to find her footing, I guess. I just don't think it's right for her to lose her dog, too. "

"I get that. I know you're always wanting to help people, and I can't really say anything because I'm the same way," Brady said.

"The problem is, I find myself thinking about her a lot. Worrying about her more than I should, considering she's really just a stranger to me. But there's just something about this woman."

"Uh-oh," Brady said. "That sounds more serious than you were letting on."

"Well, it can't be. As soon as I find her dog, she's going to take off out of town and do whatever it is that she's trying to do."

"It still sounds like you've got it bad," Brady said. "I just don't want you to open yourself up to getting hurt again."

"Yeah, I don't want that either," Jack said."I decided a long time ago that I was done dating, and that hasn't changed."

"Are you sure?" Brady asked, looking at him.

"As sure as I can be right now."

CHAPTER 8

*W*ith Jack gone to meet his friend for another search for Millie, Ava found herself sitting alone in the cabin. The silence was both anxiety-producing and comforting at the same time. She had prayed over and over that Jack would somehow find Millie, but as the days passed, she was starting to lose a little bit of her hope. The weight of the entire situation, the life that she'd fled, and the uncertainty of what was going to lie ahead pressed upon her, especially as she sat by herself.

She looked over at a bookcase that was on the side of the fireplace and noticed several photo albums stacked there with worn covers. Curiosity, and maybe an effort to distract herself from everything she was worrying about, drew her over to them. She picked one up with its soft brown leather cover under her fingers and sat on the couch with the album resting in her lap. She flipped through the pages and was transported into Jack's world. Of course, she didn't know any of the people in the photo album except for Jack, but she could tell that he was well-loved by his family.

There were pictures of him when he was younger, with a carefree and wide smile, surrounded by the beautiful landscapes of the Blue Ridge Mountains. There were pictures of family gatherings, fishing trips, bonfires, and glowing sunsets, each one was a testament to Jack's life. He had shared these moments and these memories with so many people, and yet here he was still living alone in the woods, seemingly happy with his situation. Maybe she could be like that. Maybe she too would end up alone in the end. But she had felt a growing connection to this man, who had become her unexpected protector, and maybe even her friend.

She sighed and closed the photo album, placing it back on the shelf. She wanted to know more about him, about his world, about his history, and people didn't tend to do that with strangers. There was a feeling that was starting to well within her that she was trying to push down. After all, her life was complicated enough as it was. She slipped on her coat and boots and stepped outside into the crisp air, hoping the feeling of the snow under her feet crunching would distract her from wanting to know so much more about Jack, wanting to get in too deep, and wanting to complicate her life in ways that she just couldn't afford right now.

His cabin, sitting out in the middle of a snow-covered forest, looked like something out of a story-book. She walked around, her steps truly aimless, as she took in the beauty before her. It was so quiet. The stillness of the forest was almost overwhelming. It was broken often by the sound of crows squawking in the distance.

The air was so clean and crisp and clear that it was hard to imagine breathing anything else, and the pristine snow blanketed everything in sight. It was like she was a world away from all the worries and chaos she had known, all the glare of the public eye that she had been in recently. She found a path that wound its way into the woods, and she decided to walk just a little bit, but never let the cabin get out of sight. She certainly didn't want to get lost.

She stood in the middle of the path once she was a few feet in, and found herself surrounded by the trees, looking up at the sky, which was blue without a cloud in it today. There was just something about the beauty of this place that was hard to put into words, and even though Jack lived out here alone, it didn't mean he was lonely, because he was surrounded by this all the time. This beauty and simplicity, this stark contrast to the complicated web her life had become. She understood why he loved this place, and why he had chosen to stay here, even if it meant he was alone. She made her way back toward the cabin, wondering if he had found Millie out there, if he was bringing her back. Even if he didn't, she knew he was trying his hardest, and that was really all that she could ask.

MADELINE WAS FINALLY able to venture out. The snow had stopped, and it was starting to melt just a bit with each passing hour. She wrapped her scarf tighter around her as she stepped out of her car onto the sidewalk in the town square. She just had to get to the bookstore. As an author, she spent a lot of time there herself, but she also loved to read, and she needed some new books to put on her shelf.

She opened the door, smelling the familiar scent of paper and hearing the soft sound of the instrumental music that Clemmy kept playing in the background.

"Well, if it isn't my favorite author! What made you finally venture out into the snow?" Clemmy asked.

"I had to get out of that cabin for a little bit. I guess that's what they call cabin fever," Madeline said, laughing at her joke. "Besides, I wanted to check out some of the new arrivals I saw that you got on your Facebook page."

"They are all over here on this table," Clemmy said pointing. "Couple of really good psychological thrillers in there."

They walked over to the table and Madeline picked up a couple of books, never able to resist a new release. They chatted for a few minutes before Clemmy told Madeline something that caught her attention.

"You won't believe what happened during the snowstorm. I was leaving one night during the worst of it, and this beautiful boxer dog came running down the sidewalk toward me. Jumped right in my car. She's been staying with me ever since. I even hung a flyer up on my front door in case somebody knows her owner."

"Really? Wow. Are you going to keep her if you can't find her home?"

"I've actually grown quite fond of her," Clemmy said. "But I'm worried about her owners. I know they must be missing her something fierce. Still, if I never find them, I certainly would love to keep her at my house." Clemmy showed her a photo she took on her phone. "Isn't she beautiful?"

"Yes, she is. She looks well taken care of, for sure."

They chatted for a few more minutes, and Madeline paid for her books before heading back outside. She thought about the lost dog and how she must wonder where her owners were, and they must be missing her something fierce.

As she continued walking, she saw a flyer on a lamppost down one of the side streets. It was flapping in the breeze. She assumed it might be a flyer that Clemmy had put out until she got closer. It was somebody looking for their dog. Clemmy had not been out and about much due to the snow, so she probably hadn't seen it. The dog that Clemmy had found was the same one on the flyer.

She took it down off the lamppost and turned on her heel, heading right back into the bookstore.

Clemmy looked up in surprise as she burst into the shop. Madeline held up the flyer.

"That dog you found? There are flyers all over town looking for her."

"Oh, my goodness. Really? I haven't really been walking around looking. I just put out the one here in front of the bookstore this morning. We really need to call that number immediately."

They both looked at the flyer that she grabbed, and Clemmy pulled her phone out from her pocket. As she made the call explaining the situation, Madeline was surprised that it was Jack on the other end of the line. Apparently, he was helping the woman, whose dog it was, try to find her, and Brady was out with him right then.

After hanging up, Clemmy looked at Madeline. "Thank you. I'm so glad that you found the flyer, although I'm sure I would've seen it when I walked to lunch or something. Now this pup can get back to her owner even sooner."

"Are you going to miss her?" Madeline said sticking out her lower lip a bit.

"I'm definitely going to miss her. I enjoyed the company."

"Well, then maybe we can go over to the animal shelter sometime and find you some new company,"

Madeline said smiling.

"Oh, really?" Clemmy said. "And maybe we can do the same for you because I don't remember you having a dog either."

Madeline shook her head. "Not right now. My mother is plenty to handle."

"So somebody found her?" Ava said, holding her hands together in front of her face in a prayer position. "You're not messing with me, are you?"

Jack shook his head. "Of course not. Clemmy, the bookstore owner, said Millie came bounding down the sidewalk during the snowstorm and jumped straight into her car."

"Oh, my goodness! I'm so glad she's safe," Ava said, her eyes welling with tears. She was so thankful that she was going to get Millie back in one piece. "Thank you so much for helping me put out those flyers and getting the word out. It means more than I could ever tell you," Ava said.

Without warning, she walked over and hugged Jack tightly. She had no idea what kind of zaps of electricity that was going to send throughout her body. Jack just stood there like a mountain, barely moving. She knew she had surprised him by hugging him like that, so she quickly pulled back.

"Sorry. I think I got overwhelmed with emotion."

"No problem," he said, smiling slightly. "I guess we should get in the truck and head into town so we can pick up Millie. I can't wait to meet her."

They hopped into his Jeep and took off toward the town square, pulling in front of a place called Away With Words. Ava thought it was a particularly cute name for a bookstore. She sat there in front of the store, her gaze darting back and forth, searching for any sign of Millie. Then suddenly, Clemmy was standing there in the doorway, holding a leash with Millie at the other end, who was wagging her tail with unrestrained enthusiasm. As soon as Ava saw her, she ran forward and dropped to her knees, hugging her dog tightly. Millie barked joyfully and licked her all over the face.

"Oh my Millie, I've missed you so much," Ava said, her voice choking with emotion as she buried her face in Millie's fur.

Jack stood back watching them, a smile on his face.

"Thank you so much," she said, looking up at Clemmy. "I'm so grateful that you took her in when it was that cold."

"Oh, she was a joy to have at my house. I live alone. So I loved the company for a few days."

"I'm glad to pay you back for any food you bought her or anything."

"Oh, no, no," Clemmy said, interrupting her, waving her hand. "It was no trouble really, and I hope to see her again. Will you be staying in Jubilee?"

Ava froze in place for a moment. Would she be staying in Jubilee? She supposed not. There really wasn't a reason to. But where was she going? She literally had no idea. She wasn't going back to her old life, that much was for sure.

"I'm ... I'm not quite sure yet," Ava said.

Clemmy seemed to sense her trepidation and discontinued that line of questioning. "Well, if I ever do get to see you or Millie again, I will consider it a wonderful blessing. Would you like to come into the bookstore and have a look around?"

"I appreciate it. Maybe I'll do that tomorrow. I'd like to get Millie back to the cabin, get her fed and acclimated to Jack's place. I'm sure we'll be getting out of his hair soon, though."

She couldn't quite put her finger on it, but there was a look on Jack's face, like maybe he was disappointed that she was going to leave. Surely he knew that. He wasn't expecting her to stay there forever.

"Thanks again, Clemmy," Jack said as they loaded Millie up into the Jeep.

They both climbed into the Jeep, Jack driving, Millie sitting in the back seat but standing on the console between him and Ava.

"I can't believe I have my girl back," Ava said as they drove back over the mountain.

"I'm so happy for you, Ava. I know that this has been weighing on you so much. I say we have a cele-bratory dinner tonight."

Ava smiled. "That sounds good," she said as she hugged Millie tightly and pressed her cheek into Millie's back.

Now, she felt like her life may be getting on track again. She didn't know what she was going to do or where she was going to go, but at least she had her best friend with her.

MADELINE AND BRADY sat at a cozy corner table in The Rustic Spoon, which was their favorite restau-rant in town. Madeline loved to be able to get home-cooked meals, especially if she wasn't the one who had to cook them.

Of course, Brady liked to cook, and Geneva often

brought food over, but being able to go out and let somebody else take care of the hard work was a blessing, especially on a day when they were both too tired to be in the kitchen.

"So glad that Ava got her dog back," Madeline said, taking a bite of her salad.

"Yeah, Jack was really worried about her."

"So, do you think anything is going on between those two?" Madeline asked, ever the romantic. After all, she wrote romance novels. She had to be invested in the love lives of other people. It was part of her job.

"Honestly, I think there is something blooming with them. Of course, now that she's found her dog, I don't even know if she's going to stay in Jubilee," Brady said, taking a bite of his macaroni and cheese.

"It would be really sad if they were meant to have a beautiful love story, and she had to leave town."

"I got the feeling that there's something going on behind the scenes," Brady said. "Jack sort of alluded to the fact that she was in Jubilee because she might be running away from something, so she might not want to stay here depending on what that is."

"And Jack doesn't know?"

"Not so far, or at least he didn't tell me much. I

think he has the feeling that he shouldn't pry too much with her."

"Yeah, I guess everybody has the right to their privacy, but it must be scary for her to be in town worrying that her past will catch up with her, whatever it is. You don't think she's on the run from some criminal activity, do you?" Madeline asked, chuckling under her breath.

"I don't think so. She didn't strike me as the kind who would've done something illegal from the way Jack described her to me."

"Well, we all have things that we want to run sometimes," Madeline said.

"Are you saying that you want to run from me?" Brady asked, reaching across the table and taking her hand.

"I would never run away from you," she said. "Well, unless you try to tickle me. We both know how that ends."

"I promise not to tickle you," Brady said laughing and going back to his food. "But in all sincerity, Jack really deserves a love story for the ages. He's had some serious misses with the women he's dated in the past. I really wish that he could find who he's looking for, somebody who would love him and want to be with him for the rest of his life."

"That's a very sweet thing to say," Madeline said.

"Don't tell the guys I talk that way," Brady said under his breath, as if he was whispering to her.

"Don't worry, your secret is safe with me."

AVA KNEW she should have already left Jubilee. There was really no reason to keep staying around. She had her dog, and she needed to get back on the road. The only problem was, she didn't know where the road was going to lead. She had no plan, and she certainly didn't have a lot of money to rent hotel rooms along the way.

Jack hadn't said a thing about her leaving, but she felt like she was really taking advantage of his hospitality. She knew that she was going to have to make a decision in the next couple of days. Maybe she would have to get a job somewhere and live in her truck for a bit before she could afford a place.

It wasn't that she didn't have money in her bank account. She wasn't destitute, but the first time she used her credit cards, she was going to be found. And right now, that was the last thing she wanted.

She knew that it wasn't mature of her to hide like this, but it felt like the only option. She would have to deal with the emotions of what had happened at some point.

Of course, she could call her mother for help. There was no doubt that her mom would step up and help her get on her feet again, but she was just far too embarrassed about what had happened, how she had left.

Jack offered to take her on a hike around the property. Now that the snow was almost melted, it seemed like a good thing to do, but as she stood there wearing the hiking boots that he had bought her in town the day before, she wondered if she was equipped for something like this. She had never gone on a hike in her life.

As she walked outside, the world around was still shrouded in a pre-dawn glow as she and Jack started walking. "Are you ready?" He asked. "I'm as ready as I'll ever be," she said, smiling.

The air was still crisp with each of her breaths forming a small cloud as they exhaled. She could hear her boots crunching against the frost-hardened ground. She wrapped her coat, which she had borrowed from Jack, tightly around her.

The path that he took them unwound through the towering pine trees, their branches still heavy with some of the snowfall. The forest was waking up. She could hear the sound of birds beginning to pierce the quiet. The crows were the loudest. They seemed to want to be the centerpieces of the forest world.

She sucked in a deep breath with the scent of pine and earth filling her lungs. She had never felt more grounded than when she was outside in nature in Jubilee. She noticed the smallest of details like the way that the early morning light filtered through the trees creating all kinds of shadows on the ground below, each one completely unique.

She noticed a few rabbit tracks that had crossed their path, and she could see the frost still clinging to the needles of the pine trees, making them shimmer like jewels in the sunlight.

They didn't talk much at the beginning. Jack led the way with a quiet confidence looking at her every now and then to make sure that she was okay. It wasn't a strenuous hike, especially for the mountains, but the cold did make it more challenging.

As they got to the top of the trail that he had taken them on, the sky began to turn a color of blue she had never seen before. There were streaks of pink and yellow still in the sky right on the horizon where the sunrise was moving away to give way to the light of day.

The view was breathtaking. She could see a vast expanse of forest and hills, some of which was still blanketed in snow, stretching out before them. She could also see areas where there was no snow, and the mountains looked different shades of blue.

Jack found a spot that had no snow on it and spread out a blanket he had brought. They sat down together staring off at the horizon. "What do you think?" he asked.

"I think it's one of the most beautiful things I've ever seen in my life."

She almost couldn't speak looking at it. Being able to walk out in the woods right there on his property and see something like this seemed like the biggest gift, and she was jealous of him in that moment.

"Yeah, it's one of the most beautiful places on earth. I visited a lot of places in my life, and I always wanted to come back to Jubilee, not just because of what it looks like, but because of the people that are here."

"I'm so thankful for everybody who tried to find Millie and the fact that Clemmy took care of her. I just can't thank everybody enough."

"Are you cold?" he asked. She nodded. He took another blanket that he had brought and wrapped it around her shoulders, pulling it over onto his other shoulder so that they were both under it. She could feel the heat from his body, which was a welcome contrast to the cold air around them.

Against her better judgment, she leaned into him slightly seeking warmth, but also the kind of comfort that only Jack seemed to be able to provide. They sat there in silence watching the sky and the birds. She felt like the world was holding its breath right along with her.

There was a profound sense of peace that came over her, and not only because of the view she was looking at, but because of the man beside her. She couldn't deny anymore that she had feelings for him, and it wasn't right. It wasn't okay because she was going to leave, and she didn't want to lead him on.

She didn't know if he felt the same way, but she had an inkling that he might. Ava took a glance at him when he was looking the other direction, observing his features softened by the morning light.

Just when she thought he wasn't paying attention, he suddenly turned and looked at her with an intense gaze that almost took her breath away. There were unspoken emotions hanging between them. She could tell they were on the cusp of something new, and it felt both terrifying and exhilarating.

He pulled her slightly closer to him, and she allowed herself to lean in and rest her head against his shoulder. There were no words spoken because none were necessary. Instead, they just sat there together watching the sun rise higher in the sky. She forgot all about the cold and the hiking journey. The only thing she could think about was the man sitting right next to her.

"I just can't believe how much snow is still out there," Ava said later that afternoon, as she stood at the window. Jack walked up behind her looking out as well. It looked like something straight out of a holiday card.

"Have you ever built a snowman?" he suddenly asked. She turned and looked at him, noticing his eyes sparkling a bit. A smile tugged at the corner of her lips.

"I can't say that I actually have. Is that a part of the official Jubilee winter experience that I'm supposed to be getting?"

He grinned. "Absolutely. Today seems like the perfect day for it. We have just enough leftover snow. What do you say?"

She wanted any excuse to spend more time with Jack, so she nodded. "Lead the way."

They walked outside, the cold air biting at her cheeks, but it felt invigorating to be alive in the Blue Ridge Mountains. He led her to a clearing where there was still tons of snow that hadn't melted yet, untouched and pristine.

They started by scooping up handfuls of snow, compacting it between their gloves before rolling it on the ground.

"You start with a small snowball like this, and then you just let it grow," he said. "I've done this a million times in my life."

She watched before kneeling down to start her own snowball. The snow, of course, was cold against her gloves, but it was a delightful process and something that made her feel almost childlike. Together, they rolled their snowballs across the clearing, watching them grow larger.

"Now, we need a middle section and a head," Jack called from across the way.

"Yes, I know what a snowman looks like," Ava said back, laughing.

They each worked in silence, competing with each other without saying it. Jack had brought a couple of carrots outside, so he tossed one her way.

She walked around looking for acorns to use for eyes and to form the mouth.

"This isn't bad for my first snowman," she said, sticking her chest out with pride.

"He looks pretty good, but he needs a name."

"I mean, I could go with Frosty," Ava said.

"That's really original," Jack teased.

It was then in that moment that Jack suddenly scooped up a handful of snow and made it into a ball. Before Ava could do anything, he turned to her.

"You know what else is a winter tradition around here?" She didn't get a chance to respond before he tossed a snowball and hit her right in the shoulder with it. The surprise attack ignited a spark of competition, as Ava ran behind a tree and scooped up her own snow.

A flurry of snowballs went back and forth as they each playfully dodged each other in an all out snow war. She felt alive and exhilarated by the freedom and joy of the moment. If she'd gone through with that wedding, she certainly wouldn't be doing this right now. She'd be sitting in some cold, sterile apartment in the city, wondering where her husband was and what he was doing.

But right now, she just felt like somebody having the most fun of her life. Eventually, they were both breathless and covered in snow, so they called a truce and collapsed beside each of their snowmen. In a heap of laughter, Ava looked over at Jack, his smile so genuine. She felt a warmth that had nothing to do with the sun that was peeking through the clouds overhead. There was no place else in the world that she would rather be right now, but she had to wonder if he knew her real story, would he want to spend time with her, or would he tell her to hit the road?

CHAPTER 9

*A*fter their hike earlier in the day, Ava had not been able to think about much else other than how it felt to be pressed up against Jack, to have his arm around her looking at the sunrise. With her fiance, or ex-fiance as she would refer to him now, she had never felt that way. Looking back, she couldn't even explain how she got herself into the situation. Knowing what she knew about Jack made her realize that there were men in the world who were good and kind and strong. She didn't foresee that she could ever settle for anything less than that. Even if it wasn't Jack, she would hold out for a man like him. She would hope that another one would cross her path one day, but for tonight she was going to enjoy herself. Jack had offered to give her a cooking lesson. He was going to teach her how to make his grandmother's famous apple pie.

In the cabin with the orange glow of the fireplace, they stood in the kitchen, the air filled with the sweet scent of apples and cinnamon. Ava, wearing his grandmother's apron that had little cherries embroidered all over it, was a little apprehensive as she listened to him explain the steps of the recipe. He had quite a reverence for his family's tradition.

"First, the apples," Jack said, handing her a peeler. "The trick is how you peel them. Not too thick, but not too thin."

She took the peeler and tried the first time, his hand gently covering hers, guiding her movements.

"Like this," he said, softly.

Just having his hand on hers ignited a warmth that had nothing to do with the preheating oven nearby. Their laughter filled the kitchen as flour dusted their noses and cheeks during the process of making the dough. As the pie was assembled and finally put into the oven, they started cleaning up the scattered remnants of flour around the kitchen. There was a comfortable but probably awkward silence between them that spoke volumes. Jack turned some music on, a melody from a bygone era that seemed to wrap the cabin in an embrace of nostalgia.

He extended his hand, a silent invitation asking her to dance. She accepted, her hand slipping into his as they pulled themselves closer and found a rhythm in the small space between the refrigerator and the stove. They moved together, swaying in the kitchen, their steps unscripted, but perfectly in unison. The world beyond that kitchen faded, leaving just the two of them with the music and the warmth that had enveloped them.

Ava couldn't help but look up at Jack, his eyes reflecting the soft glow of the cabin. She saw in him not just a man who had offered her shelter and friendship, but somebody that had started to fill in the spaces of her heart she didn't know were even there. The moment was tender and intimate in a way that Ava couldn't describe in words. Her heart was beating fast, and she wondered if he could feel it against his sternum.

Suddenly she noticed his gaze drop down to her lips. Slowly, as if time itself had decided to hold its own breath, he leaned down. Ava's eyes fluttered closed, and her heart felt like a jackhammer. But just as they were about to have their lips meet in probably the best kiss of her life, the oven timer dinged, the sound piercing the spell that had wrapped itself around them. They paused, their lips just inches apart, and both of them started laughing.

"Well, I guess that's our cue," Jack said, his voice husky as he cleared his throat.

They pulled apart and Ava nodded, disappointment permeating every part of her body, especially the ones that were currently tingling. He pulled the pie out of the oven, and the cabin was filled with the aroma of the baked apples and cinnamon, a sweet culmination of their effort. They looked at each other with an unspoken acknowledgement that they both knew what almost happened. That "almost kiss" lingered between them. And Ava wondered what she was getting herself into.

THE MORNING SUN was streaming through the windows of Brady's newly constructed house. It filled Anna's room with a warm, inviting light. He loved that she would wake up to this each morning before school.

Her room, which she had chosen to have

constructed with sheetrock rather than the rustic wood that was in the other rooms, was her own space that Brady had allowed her to decide how to decorate. She had chosen a vibrant shade of purple for her walls, which just went along with Anna's creativity and energy.

Madeline had put on an old pair of overalls that Brady had given her, which were way too big, but he didn't want her to ruin any of her clothes during this painting project they were taking on together. She stood beside him, holding a paintbrush and looking at the bare walls.

"Are you sure about this color?" Brady teased Madeline. "It's very purple."

Madeline laughed, dipping her brush into the paint. "It's what Anna wants. This is going to be the coolest room in the house, you just wait and see."

They worked in companionable silence as they brushed the paint against the walls. Madeline was the first to break concentration. She flung her brush from the wall onto Brady's arm, leaving a streak of that vibrant purple behind, mixed with his arm hair. Brady looked down.

"Oh, it's on now," he said, a mischievous glint in his eye. Before Madeline could do anything about it, he retaliated, plopping a dollop of purple paint right on her cheek. What had started as such a meticulous process of painting Anna's room turned into a playful fight with laughter echoing off the walls as they chased each other around the room, their brushes becoming weapons in the lighthearted battle.

In the midst of their laughter, Madeline made a daring lunge for the paint can, her hands coming away with a huge amount of paint. Brady saw what she was trying to do, so he attempted to escape, but with a triumphant laugh, she caught him and they both tumbled to the ground in a mess of painted limbs and laughter.

Brady found himself on his back, Madeline perched triumphantly on top of him, her hands poised above his forehead. She let the paint drip down, a single deliberate drop landing squarely on his forehead.

"Now you've been marked by me," she declared, letting out an evil laugh. Lying there on the floor in what would soon be Anna's dream room once they cleaned it up, surrounded by the chaos of this paint fight, they both shared a moment of pure happiness.

Madeline couldn't have ever imagined herself

doing something like this before she met Brady. She had written books with scenes like this in her life, but none of them had ever really happened to her.

They helped each other up, both of them still chuckling. "We might have gotten a little bit carried away," she said, looking around the room.

Brady reached over and wiped a smear of paint from her cheek, "Maybe, but I wouldn't have it any other way. This house is all about making new memories, right? This is a memory we'll never forget."

She hugged him tightly as she stood there looking at the walls that they needed to paint and thought about how incredibly lucky she was to have somebody who wanted to make these kinds of memories with her.

Ava couldn't believe this was the day, the day that every little girl dreams of. She would walk down the aisle and marry her prince charming and ride off into the sunset. Only she didn't feel that way. She had gotten herself into quite a predicament. She was marrying a man that she didn't really love, and she had gone so far in the process that she couldn't turn back now. Everybody knew

who she was, it seemed. Social media was talking about her and this whole spectacle that was happening today. At least she had a beautiful wedding dress.

As she stood in front of the ornate mirror in the event hall's very lavish bathroom. The reflection staring back at her didn't even look like who she thought herself to be. Yes, she was dressed in the most beautiful, expensive wedding gown, one that made her feel like a real life princess. But it felt more like a costume. A facade. It wasn't her. The fabric clung to her in all the right places. She would look beautiful in pictures later. She was sure that this video was going to be on TV very soon and all over social media, but a heaviness in her heart was weighing her down.

Around her, the bathroom was silent, a stark contrast to all the crazy bustling preparations that were going on outside in the venue. Getting ready for her to walk down the aisle. Getting prepared for a huge reception. A band setting up. Caterers everywhere. This was supposed to be the happiest day of her life, the day that she married the man of her dreams, the man that was adored by millions, but when she looked at herself in the mirror, she couldn't shake the feeling that she was making a huge mistake.

Her breath started to catch in her throat. She felt panic rising within her. She thought that this whirlwind romance that she'd had on a reality TV show had promised her love, but it was just a carefully curated illu-sion created by producers and people around her. Sure, he was a charming man, handsome even, but he was acting just as much as she was. She had realized that far too late, after he had chosen her and proposed. It was all so super-ficial. She thought maybe he was just trying to build his career at her expense. She had only been trying to build a life.

The realization that had been creeping up on her, the whispers of doubt that had been happening with each passing day had now caught up with her as she stood there looking at herself in that mirror. Would she be able to look at herself in the mirror tomorrow when she knew that she had gone through with this? Her gaze drifted over to the window. It was an escape route she hadn't even thought about until right now. Her heart raced at the thought of running away from it all, getting away from the cameras, the expectations, the social media and the marriage that felt more like a trap. She looked at herself one last time trying to decide if she could respect herself tomorrow if she was wearing a wedding ring and sitting on a beach some-where in Hawaii with a husband she didn't want. She couldn't go through with it. She couldn't marry a man she didn't love. Every fiber of her being was screaming that it was wrong.

Desperate, she lifted her dress and approached the

window. It was a small window, but she was thin and determined. She opened it up with her hands shaking, the cool air bursting through against her face. She knew climbing out was going to ruin this beautiful dress, but she did not care anymore. All that mattered was that she could escape. She climbed out so fast and didn't look back as she ran across the manicured lawns of the event hall, her heart pounding in her chest like a jackhammer. She couldn't believe she was the epitome of a rom-com movie, the bride who had escaped her own wedding.

She was heading straight to the boarding facility to pick up Millie, and that was the only clear thought in her mind. How she would explain running in with a wedding dress on would be something to worry about later, but she couldn't go without Millie by her side. She made her way through the quiet streets, through people's yards, her mind racing with plans. Where was she going? She had no idea. She just had to find somewhere to lie low and figure out the next steps in her life. Her future was completely uncertain, and maybe that would be something she liked later, but right now it felt terrifying. Even more terrifying would've been living in a loveless marriage. She had no idea what the future was going to hold, but all she knew was she had to get to her dog and her red vintage truck and everything would certainly be okay as long as she had those two things with her.

Ava suddenly awoke from an unexpected nap, her heart pounding. It seemed like every time she fell asleep, she relived that moment again. Would she ever stop thinking about it? Feeling silly and stupid and guilty? She sat up and looked out the window at Jack chopping wood, which was always a welcome sight. Why couldn't it have been him standing at that altar? She would've surely run toward him.

It seemed like Jack did nothing but split wood every day. Sometimes, he got tired of it and wanted to sleep in, but mostly he was used to this lifestyle. He stood outside hitting his axe against the wood over and over. Mainly, he just needed some time to think. This mundane task would give him just that.

All he could think about was what happened last night in the kitchen with Ava and what happened on the hike. He couldn't help himself. He needed to put his arm around her, pull her close, keep her warm. And then the "almost kiss" in the kitchen and the slow dance. The memories were both haunting and exhilarating to him. He had come so close to feeling her lips against his. He wanted to know what they felt like, but at the same time, he knew that she was probably going to be leaving town any day now. After all, there was really no reason to stay. She hadn't told him that she was at all interested in pursuing something with him, and he knew that she was trying to run from her own life.

He sat another log on the chopping block, and suddenly the scent of apple pie seemed to waft from the cabin. She must have been heating up a piece. He couldn't help but think about baking it with her and how it had felt so normal and yet so special. The laughter that they had shared. The way her eyes lit up at the simple pleasures of cooking together. Those were the moments that would always be a memory to him, whether she was still in Jubilee or not. He paused for a moment, leaning on his axe and looking at the cabin. He thought of her inside, maybe curled up with a book about to eat a piece of pie. It filled him with a longing so strong that it almost bordered on painful. He wanted her to stay. He had to admit that to himself. He wanted her to make a life here with him in Jubilee. The idea of her leaving, of the cabin going back to its quiet, solitary state felt like a dark shadow that was lingering over his home. But he knew that Ava had secrets, some kind of shadow that was lurking behind that smile. And he wanted to help her, he just didn't know how.

She was running from more than she was talking about, and he couldn't stop her from leaving. It made his chest feel tight.

He swung the axe again, the crack of the wood splitting under its weight. He wanted her to run outside to him, to see him as the protector and the haven that he was. But he feared that she would eventually leave, taking all the light that she had brought with her and leaving shadows over his heart.

Jack admitted to himself that he was worried he might get heartbroken with this one. He had opened up to her in ways he hadn't with anyone in a long time, and yet sitting with her quietly felt just as intimate as talking. This had all been such a gamble, and there was a really good chance he was about to lose.

He finished splitting the last log and gathered the wood, stacking it neatly nearby. For some reason, he felt like this risk had been worth it. Every moment he had spent with her, every smile, every laugh, even every shared look had been worth the risk. She had brought him warmth during this cold winter time, and maybe she had given him hope that it was possible to fall in love with somebody who loved him back just as much.

He stood there staring at the cabin once more, a

resolve setting over him. He was going to cherish the time that he had with her and make the most of every moment. He was going to show her what it was like to have a strong, solid man beside her. And maybe when it came time for her to face the decision of staying or going, she would make the decision that would change his life for the better.

AVA COULDN'T BELIEVE how the mundane parts of domestic living felt so important to her right now. The hum of the washing machine filled Jack's small laundry room, and she absently folded a towel, her movements as automatic as if she had been doing it for years.

She stared out the window, watching Jack as he finished stacking wood, his movements so sure and fluid. She loved to watch him swing that axe, although she would never tell him so. It showed such strength and capability, and the sight of him sent an unexpected shiver down her spine. He was undeniably attractive. And as she watched him work with the way his muscles moved under his shirt with the occasional glint of sweat on his brow, she couldn't help but admire him and feel attracted to him.

He had been so warm to her since the moment she arrived. Her hands had stopped as she forgot about the towel in her lap and watched him. There was a sense of longing mixed with regret that tugged at her heart. She had no real reason to stay in Jubilee any longer. Millie was safe and sitting at her feet. Every day that she was there, she felt like she was supposed to leave, like there was really no reason to keep stringing him along. She was taking advantage of his good nature, and it had to stop, sooner rather than later.

But the thought of leaving this place, of leaving Jack, made her feel like she had already lost everything. Tonight, she decided, she would tell him at dinner that she needed to leave, not only to protect herself from Jack, but from her past coming to find her. Well, maybe she wouldn't tell him that last part.

The realization that she had to tell him she was leaving felt like a weight on the top of her shoulders, her head, and in her heart, especially. He didn't know her full story, and if she had her way, he never would. She didn't want him to ever look at her differently with regret or pity. It was something she just couldn't bear.

She forced herself to look away from the window and get back to the task at hand, but her mind was drifting elsewhere, dreading the conversation to come. How do you tell someone goodbye who has been the greatest beacon of light in your darkest time? How do you walk away from a place that, for the first time ever, feels like home?

The washing machine beeped, startling her, but the sound seemed so distant and inconsequential to the racing of her heart. She finished folding the towels and sat there a moment longer than she needed to because as every moment passed, she was faced with the inevitable conversation. Dinnertime was approaching, and she felt such a sense of dread.

She had tried to rehearse what she was going to say, how she was going to tell him thank you, and explain her need to leave. Every scenario made her feel despair. This was not going to be easy for her or for Jack.

Dinner was a quiet affair. The tension was palpable. She watched Jack, the way he moved around the kitchen and would occasionally smile in her direction. It struck her just how much she had come to care for him, how her own happiness had been mixed with his presence. Untangling herself from this life that she had led for the past few days was going to be so much more painful than she could have ever anticipated.

When they finished dinner and were sitting there with the remnants of their meals between them, Ava finally took in a deep breath. This was it. She was going to tell him that she was leaving, and that would be that.

"Jack," she began, her voice barely above a whisper, "I need to tell you something very important." He looked at her, waiting for what she was going to say, but then before she could get the words out, he interrupted.

"I have an idea."

JACK KNEW what she was going to say, and he just wasn't going to allow it. Before she could even get the words out, he interrupted her. He knew it was the wrong thing to do, to make her wait even longer to tell him the inevitable news that she was leaving town, but he couldn't stand it. He needed one more night with her in his cabin beside him, bringing a smile to his face.

It was a beautiful, clear night where the fabric of the sky seemed to be embroidered with a thousand stars. Jack led Ava out to his pickup truck where he had set up blankets and pillows and strung twinkle lights around the edges.

"What is this?" Ava said, as he pulled her hand outside.

"I just thought that maybe we could enjoy a night under the stars."

She looked up. "I have never seen the sky so clear. In the city, you can't see stars like this." She seemed to be truly amazed.

"Are you warm enough?" he asked, having given her his thickest coat.

She nodded. "Yeah, it's not so bad out here tonight."

"Let me help you up," Jack said holding his hand out, as she climbed up into the bed of the truck. Although the air was a little cooler than the warmth the day had finally turned into, it wasn't frigid. The promise of spring was just around the corner. Or maybe it was just another example of a blackberry winter in Georgia.

Many of the locals knew that it would get warm and trick you into thinking that spring was coming, but then you'd get another cold snap. They were in that in-between stage where it felt like spring was coming, but it probably wasn't for at least a few more weeks. He climbed in behind her, and they laid down side by side, looking straight up at the stars.

Jack pulled a thick blanket over them and made sure that she had a pillow under her head. He couldn't imagine this being the only time he ever got to do this with Ava. Her beautiful red hair flowed out behind her, and the moon seemed to shine on it in a way that it lit up. He could hardly keep himself from staring at her, so he quickly turned his attention back to the sky.

It felt like they were in their own secluded sanctuary, where nobody could ever get to them. Jack pointed out constellations, his arm brushing against Ava's as he traced patterns in the sky with his finger. She listened intently, turning her head, laughing when he said something funny or silly.

The stars seemed to cast a spell over them as the night deepened and the darkness became a canvas for the stars. Ava talked about dreams that she'd kept hidden, her voice a whisper against the backdrop of an infinite sky. Jack talked about some of his own hopes and dreams, like building more structures on the property and maybe retiring from private security altogether. He had plenty of money saved, and he owned his property. All he needed now was someone to share it all with, but he left that part out.

He seldom shared these thoughts with anyone, but there was a quiet understanding of something beautiful blooming between them. It seemed like hours had slipped by, and a shooting star carved a brief brilliant path across the sky in front of them.

"Make a wish," Jack said quietly. Ava closed her eyes, a smile curving at her beautiful, full lips. When she opened her eyes, he was looking at her, and they held that gaze for a long moment. Slowly, as if drawn by some force beyond both of their control, they each turned to face each other, their eyes locked. There was a silence between them that was charged with anticipation.

Jack reached out his hand, gently cupping her face, his thumb brushing against her cheek. His heart raced in his chest, which didn't often happen, given his history of law enforcement. He had to stay cool as a cucumber under very stressful circumstances. But with Ava, nothing fell into the rule book.

The world around them faded, and he had nothing else to do but press his lips to hers. He leaned in and closed the distance between them, and in a moment felt her lips against his. The kiss was gentle and tentative, a question asked and answered at the same time.

As the kiss deepened, Jack couldn't feel anything else around him except Ava's lips. The warmth and connection was almost overpowering. He knew the kiss felt like possibilities, a hope for something, a new beginning, and he couldn't bear to tell himself that this kiss could actually be goodbye.

CHAPTER 10

*A*va was curled up on the couch with a book in her hand when a knock at the door broke the silence. She thought maybe it was Jack forgetting his keys or some kind of delivery coming. She knew he had gone into town for some supplies, so she didn't really know who else to expect way out in the remote wilderness this early in the morning.

She was surprised to open the door and find Geneva standing there. She had only met her briefly in town, but she had heard a lot about Geneva from Jack. She was like everybody's mother, or maybe even grandmother, in town. She'd been there forever. She knew everything about the area, and she seemed to be slightly in everybody's business, although they all seemed to love it.

"Good morning, Ava," Geneva said, her voice as comforting as the scent of the pine trees surrounding the cabin. "I was just passing by and thought you might enjoy some company. Is Jack out?"

Ava was a little bit taken aback by the gesture. How in the world did Geneva know that Jack was out, and who was passing by on this remote mountain road?

"Yes, he went into town for some supplies. Come on in. I'd love the company."

Geneva had a large thermos of coffee in her hand. She walked into the kitchen like she'd been there a million times and pulled two mugs from the shelf, pouring coffee in both of them. She handed one to Ava and then sat down at the breakfast table. Ava figured that was a hint that she was supposed to sit down too.

"So what brings you out here?" Ava asked.

"Well, I actually might have told a fib. I knew Jack wasn't here. I did see him in town a bit ago. I thought I might catch you alone for a few minutes."

"Okay. Is something wrong?"

"No. I just must admit that when I recognized you in town, I felt like I was a little short with you.

Maybe I didn't welcome you to Jubilee in the proper way."

"Oh, no. I didn't feel that way at all," Ava said. "I was very appreciative that you kept my secret. I still haven't told Jack everything, and that makes me feel terrible. But what's worse would be him judging me or thinking less of me for being on a reality TV show looking for love. It's pretty embarrassing."

"Well, we all have things in our lives that are embarrassing from time to time," Geneva said. She had very kind eyes, and Ava appreciated her soft approach.

"I don't know what got into me when I made that decision. My mother tried to warn me, and I just went through with it. I think I was just so ready to find my person, you know?"

"Oh, yes, dear. I understand. I had my person for decades before he passed away. I know how important it is to find the right one."

"Well, certainly going on a reality show was not the best way to go about it," Ava said. "And climbing out the window in my wedding dress was probably not the best idea either. It was so beautiful, but by the time I made it to my vehicle, it looked like somebody had ripped it to shreds."

"Oh, dear," Geneva said, chuckling.

"It's definitely not a part of my life that I'm proud of. The show was sort of the culmination of years of wanting something that I just couldn't find. Then when I got on the show, I realized the manipulation that goes on with these types of TV programs, the constant surveillance, and then the aftermath. The bullying on social media was relentless."

Geneva reached across the table, squeezing her hand, "I'm so sorry, dear. That sounds terrible. The world can be so cruel, especially when it feels like your misery is everybody else's entertainment. I have to say, I'm so glad I didn't grow up in that era of social media. I don't know how you young kids handle it."

Ava smiled and nodded. "Thank you for thinking of me as a young kid."

Geneva waved her hand, "Oh, dear. You're very much a young kid compared to me."

"It was a terrible time on that show. I just felt so lost and so disconnected from who I really am. Since I got here to Jubilee, since I met Jack, I'm starting to feel like myself again, but I won't get to stay here. I have to leave now that I've found my dog."

"You're braver than you know, Ava. You escaped something that wasn't for you. You took off and started over not even knowing where you were going. You just have to remember that you're not alone, that you have people here who would care about you. You have a community that would surround you and become like family."

"Thank you. I've been so scared of being judged, of dragging my past into this place, this quiet, calm place that Jack has created. I don't want to do that to him."

"Everyone has a past, my dear," Geneva said, "It's what we do with the time that we have right now that matters the most. You can redefine yourself anytime you want, on your own terms. And as for those bullies, they only have the power that you give them. You hold your head up high, you live your truth, and you let your actions just speak for themselves.

They talked for quite a long time, Geneva sharing all kinds of stories about the history of Jubilee, tales of the Appalachian Mountains, and even some of the work that she did taking people on nature hikes. Ava felt like she had made a new friend, and she understood why everybody seemed to love Geneva.

"Thank you so much for coming by, Geneva, and for the coffee. But most of all, for the company and the wisdom," she said as she walked her to the door.

"Anytime, dear," Geneva said, stepping back out

into the crisp winter air. "And you remember, no matter if you're here or not, you're a part of Jubilee, and we look out for our own."

AFTER THE KISS they shared in the truck, Ava could hardly think of anything else. The kissing had gone on for quite some time before they went inside, each of them going to their rooms.

She wondered if Jack had slept. She certainly hadn't. He had to get up early to run errands that morning, so she was at the cabin alone for quite a while even after Geneva left. Jack said they would meet up later at dinner.

All that she could think about was that kiss. She had never felt anything like it in her entire life. It wasn't like she had kissed tons of people, but certainly none of them had the skills Jack did. He had made her feel things deep down in her soul that she didn't even know were possible.

She had no idea how she was ever going to leave town. How could she ever walk away knowing that she would never find this again? It seemed unique. It seemed like a one of a kind love. She had to admit to herself that's what she felt for Jack, even after just these few days. She felt *love*. She was never going to tell him that, of course. It was too embarrassing to admit.

She had no idea if he felt the same. But even if he did, she wasn't going to be the one to break his heart. As the day unfolded, and it got closer to dinnertime, Jack finally showed up back at the cabin. He smiled as he jumped out of the truck and told her he was going to go change clothes and then they could go eat dinner. He was taking her to a place called The Rustic Spoon, which she had seen on the town square.

She had decided that tonight would be the night that she needed to tell him she was leaving. It was going to be the hardest conversation she'd ever had. Maybe one day she'd date again, and now she knew what she was looking for - someone who had her back. Someone who was kind and gentle, yet strong. Someone who made her laugh. Someone who made her tingle from head to toe with just a look.

They drove to The Rustic Spoon, and their table was a small round one on the side of the restaurant, lit by the soft glow of a candle that flickered between them. The menu was a testament to all the local flavors, and she couldn't wait to have some good southern cooking.

She chose chicken and dumplings, a side salad, and some sweet tea. As they talked, Ava tried to figure out how to broach the conversation, how to tell Jack that she had to leave. How to tell the man that made her feel truly seen for the first time in her life, that she was going to move on.

"You know it's strange," she said, twirling her fork in her hand, "how this place that I never knew existed feels like home. I feel more like myself here than I have in my whole life."

He smiled and reached across the table, gently squeezing her hand. "Jubilee has a way of doing that. I'm just glad it brought you here."

Why had she said such a thing? Why had she admitted that it felt like home? It was just going to make this so much harder.

Before she could tell him, Madeline and Brady walked over and said, hello.

"We didn't expect to see you two here tonight," Madeline said.

"Oh, just enjoying all that our little town has to offer," Jack said.

"Make sure you try the pie, it's almost as good as Jack's," Brady said to Ava.

They each laughed and chatted for a few moments before Madeline and Brady excused themselves to go to their own table. It was the perfect evening, and Ava hated to ruin it with her news. Just as she was about to tell Jack what her plans were, the door opened, and she noticed an unexpected figure stepping through. She couldn't believe her eyes. Her stomach wanted to jump out through her mouth.

It was Landon Chase. Her fiancé. Everybody turned around. Most of the country knew exactly who he was. Famous son of a famous TV producer. Uber wealthy. Full of himself. And star of the reality TV show, "Luxury Love Match", where he dated a dozen women and then chose one to marry. And somehow, he chose her. She still didn't really know why.

At first, he'd seemed nice enough. The idea of traveling the world with a handsome, wealthy man was tantalizing at first, especially since Ava had worked as a hair stylist for years. She wasn't exactly making millions and traveling the globe. She felt silly now that she'd even thought to apply for the show, much less allow herself to get engaged.

There was a camera crew maneuvering behind Landon, capturing the moment. Ava thought she was going to pass out at the sight of him here, in this place that became her sanctuary. He didn't fit in at all.

There was nowhere to go, nowhere to run. The cameras, the lights, they were as undeniable as the reality of her past crashing right into her present.

Jack noticed the sudden shift in her demeanor and looked at the door, his expression hardened as he took in the scene.

"Ava?" Jack said. But Ava could barely hear him over the rush of panic and her own heartbeat pounding in her ears. She felt exposed, raw.

The Rustic Spoon, which was a cozy setting for her just moments ago, suddenly felt like a stage, and she was unwillingly standing in the spotlight at its center.

Landon's eyes found her. He looked surprised, satisfied, and then maybe even a little possessive. The camera crew fanned out to capture every angle, every reaction. This was why she had not wanted to marry him in the first place; it had all been too much from the very beginning.

Everybody in the room turned to witness the unfolding drama seeming to forget their own meals, including Madeline and Brady. The camera came closer to Ava's shocked face. This was going to be great reality television. She tried not to look at Jack, not wanting to see the disappointment on his face. The confusion, the anger. She hadn't told him this part. She hadn't told him exactly how she met her fiancé.

THE MOMENT A MAN walked through the door with a camera crew, Jack could tell that something had gone wrong with Ava. She looked like she was frozen. She couldn't bear to be sitting there. He wanted to pick her up and run out of the restaurant with her. He had such a protective instinct, but he also wanted to know what was going on. Who was this guy and what was he doing here, especially with cameras? Jack sensed the gravity of the situation, so he instinctively stood up, his posture protective. This is what he did. He protected people. It was his job.

"Landon, what are you doing here?" Ava's voice was steady, but he could hear it shaking slightly.

Landon seemed to be ever the charmer in front of the cameras and flashed a smile.

"Ava, darling, I've been looking everywhere for you. Imagine my surprise when I stood down at the front of the church and didn't find you there in a wedding dress. Instead, you're here in this quaint little town."

Jack was confused. What were these cameras doing here? "You need to leave, man. She doesn't want you here."

"And you are?"

"None of your business," Jack said, staring him down.

"Do you know who I am?"

"Nope."

"I'm Landon Chase. I'm surprised that you don't know me." He looked at the camera and shrugged his shoulders.

"Why would I know you?" Jack asked.

"Well, because I'm pretty well known on television."

"I don't watch television," Jack said, crossing his arms.

"And who might you be again?" Landon asked, looking him up and down.

"I'm someone who cares about Ava's well-being, which is more than I can say for you right now. So turn off these cameras and leave her alone."

Jack's voice was more of a growl, barely containing his anger. The tension between the two men crackled in the air. Jack wanted to lay him out on the floor. The camera crew sensed the escalating drama and moved closer trying to capture every moment. Landon was unfazed by Jack's protective stance and turned his attention back to Ava.

"Wow, seems like you moved on pretty quickly, Ava. I'm willing to forgive you if you just come back with me. We have a life to get back to, some commitments that you need to fulfill. You can't hide away in this little place forever."

"Landon, I'm not coming back. My life is my own, and I'm not going to live it in front of these cameras anymore."

He seemed amused by her response. "You'll come around, Ava. You always do. After all, you agreed to get engaged, knowing that this was what our life would be."

Jack stepped forward between them, his entire body tense. "She said she's not going back. You need to respect it and leave now. This is your final warning."

Landon's smirk faltered a bit. Ava placed a hand on Jack's arm.

"Jack, please. Let's not make this any worse. I just want him to leave." Jack relaxed slightly, but then turned his gaze back to Landon.

"This isn't over, Ava," Landon said, looking around Jack before signaling for the crew to follow him.

As the door closed behind them, there seemed to be a collective sigh in the restaurant. Jack turned to Ava.

"Are you okay?"

Her adrenaline level must have been at the maximum.

"I will be. Thank you for standing up for me. I don't know what I would've done without you."

But Jack was angry. He was angry that Ava hadn't shared the full story with him. That she had somehow been engaged on a reality TV show didn't seem like the person he knew. Maybe he had never really known her at all.

THE DRIVE back to Jack's cabin was basically silent. There was a space between Ava and him that was full of unasked questions. She could tell that his mind was racing, probably trying to piece together how he felt and torn between defending a woman he barely knew against a crew of cameras. When they arrived and stepped out into the cool night air, Ava felt so much sadness in her gut. She was bracing herself for words that Jack was going to say. She tried to stop him from starting the conversation by starting it herself.

"Jack, I just want to say…" Ava began, but he held up a hand stopping her.

"Not now. I need some time to think." He walked into his bedroom and closed the door behind him, leaving her standing alone in the living room.

It felt so final, like a silent confirmation that whatever was starting between them was over. She knew that she had done the wrong thing by not telling him the full story, but how embarrassing would it have been to share with this man who she had formed a connection with that she had let herself get involved in some silly reality TV show.

She knew that she was going to have to leave Jubilee, leave Jack, leave this promising relationship, all because of her own stupid mistakes. She sat down on the sofa and just stared straight ahead at Jack's book cases. She was looking at absolutely nothing. It was like she was waiting for the school principal to open his door and call her in like she had gotten into big trouble.

She couldn't remember a time in her life when her heart had felt as heavy. Even running away from her own wedding hadn't felt like this. Even the moment on the side of the road when she thought she might lose her life in the cold, snowy mountains, she hadn't felt this sad.

Never having really been in love meant that when you lost something, it didn't hurt as much. But now that she felt like she was falling in love with Jack, it felt like she was losing everything. Millie, sensing that she was upset, curled up at her feet, and Ava leaned down to pet her head. She was so thankful that even though she had lost her dog for a while, she had come back unharmed. She could only hope that even though she felt like she was losing Jack right now, that somehow things would turn around.

"Boy, that was something else. I can't stop thinking about Ava and Jack," Madeline said, as she sat on her sofa with her knees pulled up to her chest, a blanket wrapped around her.

Brady sat at the other end, his elbows on his knees, facing the fireplace. "Yeah. What happened tonight was shocking, to say the least. I don't think I've ever even seen a camera crew come through Jubilee."

"I never would've guessed that Ava was involved

in something like that. And poor Jack. He looked so stunned. He stood up for her, but you could tell he was having a real problem with the information that guy was giving him. I feel for him. I really do," Madeline said.

The arrival of Ava's fiance, Landon Chase, with that camera crew had turned a simple dinner in Jubilee into a spectacle that nobody was prepared for.

"It must have been really hard for her to have her past show up like that for everybody in town to see," Brady said. "And in front of Jack no less. I know he has feelings for her, I just wonder what he's feeling right now."

"He's a good guy. He's been nothing but supportive of her since she arrived, from what I understand. And to find out in such a public way, that's got to hurt."

They sat there in front of the fire for a while, quietly thinking through the situation. "Do you think they'll get through this?" Brady asked, looking over at Madeline.

"I hope so. They seem like they're good together, but I don't know if he's going to be able to accept the fact that she's in the public eye like that."

"Yeah, he's a pretty private guy. He likes being by himself out in those woods."

"I don't think he really likes being by himself," Madeline said, smiling slightly. "I think he has enjoyed having her there."

"Yeah, but he loves living a private life. And Jack's always been that way. He has always gone home to those woods, even when he was a deputy. And the fact that she's bringing so much publicity into his world, I just don't know if he'll be able to take that."

"I just wish there was something we could do to help them," Madeline said.

Brady reached over and squeezed her hand gently. "Being there for them is the best we can do. And hope that whatever love or feelings have brewed between them is strong enough to withstand this storm."

THIS SEEMED like the longest night of her life. Ava had gone into her bedroom for a while to get changed and get ready for bed, but she knew there was going to be no sleep.

As she walked past her window, she noticed the fire pit lit up and Jack sitting beside it alone, the orange glow of the flames casting a soft light over his face. He had a cup of coffee between his hands and looked like he was lost in thought. Her heart clenched, knowing that this conversation could be the last one.

She took a deep breath to steady herself and then walked outside.

"Jack?"

He looked up at her, his expression very guarded.

"Ava," he said, his tone neutral.

"Can we talk?"

He nodded, pointing to a log across from him. She had loved sitting next to the fire with him for the short time they'd known each other. She was going to miss this.

She took a seat, and the warmth of the fire did very little to ease the chill that had settled between them. Ava sat there for a moment trying to gather her thoughts, searching for the right words.

"I owe you an explanation about, well, pretty much everything, especially about the show and why I was on it."

He remained silent, still staring at the fire, giving her a chance to speak.

"When I signed up for that show, I was lost, Jack.

Before Jubilee, before meeting you, well, my life really wasn't going anywhere. I'm not a writer."

"Lie number one, I guess," he said under his breath.

"I'm a hairstylist. I was barely making ends meet, and I heard about this reality show. I thought what did I have to lose?"

"Your dignity and self-respect, maybe?"

"I know that now, but I didn't think that far ahead. I guess I thought it would be a memorable experience. I signed up for this show thinking it would give me a sense of direction, a sense of purpose. Maybe it would be something fun. Maybe I would meet the love of my life, but I was wrong. It was all just an illusion and one that I almost bought into until it was too late."

She looked at his eyes hoping for understanding, but she saw nothing yet.

"I never loved Landon. The engagement and the wedding, it was all for the cameras. I realized that I couldn't marry someone that I didn't love and live a lie for the rest of my life, and so that's why I ran. I didn't even have a plan. I just took off, and I ended up here in Jubilee with you."

He finally looked at her.

"Why didn't you just tell me all of this before?"

"I was terrified. I was afraid you'd see me as just some kind of reality TV star and not the person that I actually am or the person that I want to be. I didn't want to lose the one good thing that's happened to me in so long. What you don't understand is that when you get involved with a TV show like this, you blow up on social media. People say all kinds of hurtful things about you. They talk about your body, your face, your personality. They make up lies. People that you never really even knew come out of the woodwork to tell stories about you that never happened. It all got to be too much for me, and I couldn't lean on Landon, not at all. He was very interested in just getting more famous. I was not."

Her confession just hung in the air like a fragile bridge made of fog spanning the distance between them.

He sighed, setting his coffee on a stump beside him.

"Ava, I'm not going to pretend that I'm not hurt. I really thought I knew you. I thought you had told me almost everything. I never imagined a camera crew would interrupt dinner and put me on TV when I never wanted to be. I thought I had made it easy for you to confide in me, but I understand why you did it, I guess. It just doesn't mean I'm okay with how I found out."

She nodded, accepting his words and acknowledging his pain.

"I know, and I'm so sorry. You have been nothing but kind and supportive, and I've taken that for granted."

He shook his head. "No, you haven't."

She took in a deep breath, not wanting to say the next words that were going to come out of her mouth.

"I want to thank you, Jack, for everything, but I'm leaving tomorrow. It's not right for me to stay here. Not after all of this."

"Ava, I..." he trailed off, his conflict evident. "I don't want you to go because of this. What we've shared has been real for me, despite how we got here. Does that not count for anything to you?"

"It does, Jack, more than you know, but I need to do this. I need to find my way in the world without running. I don't want my past catching up with me to hurt you more than it already has. And the truth is, this doesn't end now just because I am not marrying Landon. Just because I left a reality TV show. I'm forever known on social media as the runaway bride, and you don't need that in your life."

They sat there in silence for a few more moments before Ava stood.

"Goodnight, Jack. I just want you to know you've given me more than you'll ever know."

She walked inside and quietly shut the door behind her, going into her bedroom and falling onto the bed, trying to muffle her cries.

CHAPTER 11

*J*ack tossed and turned all night. His
conversation with Ava had left him
feeling so conflicted. He certainly
didn't want to stop her from leaving if that's what
she wanted to do, and a part of him wondered if he
would be able to handle a life with a woman who
was constantly going to be stalked by random
strangers on the internet. Of course, he was trained
for that, but did he want to spend his life worrying
about what other people said about her and about
their relationship online?

As the first light of dawn finally crept across the
horizon, peeking through his window blinds, Jack
got up and sat on the side of his bed. Normally at
this time of the morning, he would hear Millie

running around in the living room, waiting for somebody to fill up her bowl. It was amazing how quickly he had become accustomed to having both of them in his house. A once quiet place all the time, there was life in it, and if she left, he was going to miss that. He stood up, stretched and opened the door, walking out into the living room, but there was no sign of anyone. Surely she hadn't left this early. Waking up to silence in the cabin again was a stark contrast to the warmth and companionship that had filled its rooms for so many days.

He walked into the kitchen and found a note on the table, the handwriting on it shaky. It was an apology and a thank you all rolled into one.

DEAR JACK,

I'm sorry I left without saying a proper goodbye. I just couldn't do it. I guess it shows my cowardly nature. My inclination to run when things get hard. But that's not what this is. I know if I tried to say goodbye, I couldn't. I'd want to stay, and you'd try to get me to stay.

What I want for you more than anything is happiness. Please get out there and meet someone who deserves you. Someone who deserves a life in your cozy cabin. Someone who deserves fun nights cooking in the kitchen and long hikes at sunrise. Someone who deserves slow dancing while a pie cooks and kissing in the back of your truck.

I thought that was me until I saw those cameras. I've made a mess of my life, and I hope I can get back to some semblance of normal one day. I'll miss you, Jack. And Millie will, too.

Thank you for being my protector and refuge when I needed it most.

Love,

Ava

HE COULDN'T BELIEVE IT. She was gone. Just to make sure, he looked out the front door and noticed her truck was missing. He didn't know when or if he would ever see her again, and the thought made him feel sick at his stomach. He should have fought harder. He should have said more, but he was so shocked and hurt that he just needed a good night of sleep. This morning, he had planned to have a conversation to try to see if there was any way to work this out, but now it wouldn't matter because he had no idea where she was.

He decided to drive into town and get a cup of coffee. Even the town seemed quieter as he made his way to Perky's to have a little breakfast and coffee.

As he was sitting there drinking a cup and staring into it, Geneva came in. She looked at him with a knowing glance and came and sat down across from him.

"Morning, Jack," she said. "You look like you've lost something precious."

He managed a weak smile. "You could say that, I guess. Ava, she left this morning."

"Oh, yes, I heard. I had watched her quite a bit on TV."

He stared at her. "Wait, you knew? Why didn't you tell me?"

"Because I made a promise. I spoke to Ava one time in town and told her I knew who she was, and I promised that I wouldn't share it with anyone. She needed to deal with it in her own time."

"I guess you heard what happened at dinner."

"I did. Things happen."

"Things happen?" he said, laughing. "That wasn't just a thing. That was something most people will never have to go through."

"That's true, and I'm sorry, Jack. I know that it must have been very embarrassing and upsetting. But let me tell you if there's one thing I've learned in my years, it's that real love is worth fighting for. It's worth not only giving the other person grace, but giving yourself that, as well."

He sighed. "I don't even know where to start. She didn't just leave, Geneva. She ran from something she thought she wanted only to find herself caught between what we started to build here and her past. How do I fight for that? How do I convince her that what we have is worth staying for? How do I know she wouldn't just eventually run away from me?"

She reached across the table and covered his hand. "You're never going to be one-hundred percent certain that somebody isn't going to leave, but if you give her something worth staying for, then why would she? You both deserve that chance, Jack. Don't let fear or pride stand in your way of mending what's been broken."

"And if she's already made up her mind? If she's already long gone?" Jack said.

"Well, I believe that there's always a moment where everything wrong can be made right, and if you speak to her, at least she'll know that you tried. Life's too short for what-ifs, Jack. You have to check out every path to see where it might lead."

She patted his hand one more time and got up, walking to the cash register to get her own cup of coffee. Jack sat there wondering what to do. How would he even find her to talk to her? But he had a newfound sense of resolve. At least he could travel all those roads to see if she was on any of them, and he would know that he had tried.

IT WAS a tranquil morning in the park in Jubilee, where the whispers of nature blended with the laughter of children. Burt stood there in his normal spot, years of dedication calling him there each morning to feed the wildlife. Everybody in town knew him. He'd been doing this for well over a decade now. The birds, the squirrels, the chipmunks, and any sort of wildlife would approach him without any fear.

Eloise stood there watching in awe as a cardinal, beautiful in its crimson splendor, fluttered down to rest on his hand, pecking gently at seeds he held in his open palm. Around his feet, squirrels were scampering and tussling, vying for the peanuts that he had thrown down. It was a scene straight out of a storybook. Eloise couldn't help but stare at him, plus she found him to be quite handsome.

"You see," Burt said, "they know me. They know

that I mean no harm. It's all about trust, patience and being still."

"Do you think I could try?" she asked, a mix of nervousness in her voice. It wasn't like he was going to allow her to be pecked in the eyes by birds, but she still felt a little scared, nonetheless.

"Of course," Burt said. He guided her to stand beside him, telling her to hold her hand flat and still, and then put a few seeds in it. "Now just relax and give in to the moment. They will sense if you're calm."

She took a deep breath, trying to steady her trembling hand. Age would do that to a person. She held it up toward the sky. Everything around them seemed quiet at that moment. At first, nothing happened, and she was kind of disappointed. But Burt, who was a very patient teacher, whispered, "Patience, Eloise. Just breathe and wait."

She took his advice to heart and then focused on the warmth of the sun on her face as she closed her eyes. She could hear the gentle rustle of leaves in the breeze and smell the soft, earthy scent of the creek next to them. Her nerves settled and peace enveloped her. And then almost like magic, a small bird, curious and bold, came down and landed right on her hand. She could feel its tiny little feet. She opened her eyes and saw it looking at her as it pecked at the seeds. It was the most amazing thing she had ever witnessed.

Burt had a proud smile on his face. A squirrel who was emboldened by the quiet, calm atmosphere, scampered over to her leg and waited for her to lean down to hand it a peanut. Just as a little bird flew away, she leaned down and gave the squirrel the nut.

She laughed. "I can't believe it. They really trust me."

"It's a beautiful thing, isn't it?" Burt said. "Having this moment of connection every day with the creatures in this park always reminds me to appreciate the simple joys in life."

They stood there together, looking out over the creek, and Eloise felt such a sense of gratitude that she had found Jubilee, that she had reconnected with her daughter, and that she had started to form a connection with this man. All of these were blessings and miracles in her life.

As Jack left the coffee shop, the realization hit him like a thunderstorm. His heart raced with urgency and regret. How had he let her leave so easily? Why hadn't he fought?

For so many years, he had wanted to fall in love again. To have someone there with him in that quiet forest. And now that he knew what that felt like, he didn't want to lose it, but she was gone. He didn't even know what time she left. She could have been gone for hours as far as he knew. She could have been in another state by now. He didn't even have her cell phone number, and it was likely she didn't have it turned on, anyway. How had he allowed this to happen?

As he hurriedly made his way back to his truck, the engine roaring to life, he set off down all the winding roads of Jubilee. He didn't even know where he was going, much like when Ava had arrived in town in the first place. His mind was racing as fast as the vehicle, so he had to stop for a moment and think. If she was leaving town, which road would she have taken? Where was she most likely to be?

He drove with purpose, his eyes scanning every turn and every road for any sign of the woman he loved. There was a scenic overlook that he thought maybe she would've stopped at to take a rest, to take some pictures, to say goodbye to Jubilee. It was a remote possibility, but he had to check it out. So, he went down the road heading towards the scenic overlook and up the mountain. Maybe she had sought solace and peace at that place one last time.

As he approached the overlook, his heart leaped at the sight of her truck sitting there. Unmistakably broken down, the hood was popped. Ava stood beside it, looking like she was lost and had no idea what to do. Her posture was one of defeat, and he was so happy that he was going to get to save her one more time. He was desperately relieved. As he pulled up beside her, she turned and looked at him, surprise etched on her face.

He stepped out and leaned against his Jeep. "Got a problem?"

"I think that's pretty obvious," she said, putting her hands on her hips. "I've been standing here for over an hour. Doesn't anybody drive down this road?"

He smiled slightly as he walked toward her. "Not often."

"How did you know where I was?"

"I didn't. I've been driving around for a bit, but then I thought maybe you might take this route out of town," he said as he got closer to her.

"Why are you here, Jack?"

"Ava, I can't let you leave. Not like this."

"I think it's better this way. After everything that's happened, I don't think you would want…"

"Don't tell me what I would want," he interrupted. "Yes, I was shocked last night. I wasn't expecting a *camera crew* to be in my face, and I really wanted to punch that guy out." She chuckled under her breath.

"Yes, I could tell."

"The truth is, I'm not scared of a stupid camera crew. I'm not scared of an idiot reality TV guy. I've never been scared of much of anything, Ava. But, I'm scared of never seeing you again. I'm scared of losing you. That's what scares me. I have feelings…"

"What do you mean by feelings, Jack?"

Should he say the words? It was so early. They hadn't known each other all that long.

"I don't know what to say…"

"Well, that's not enough for me. I'm sorry. I've already been in a relationship with somebody that I didn't share the same feelings for. I don't want to do that again."

He turned and looked behind him. His hands on his hips, almost annoyed at this conversation before he turned back to her.

"So, wait, are you saying you're not in love with me, too?" Her mouth dropped open.

"You're in love with me?"

"Well, I thought that much was obvious."

She started laughing. "It's not obvious, Jack. It's never obvious if somebody's in love with you unless you say the words."

"We've only known each other a short time. It feels silly to say I love you already."

She shrugged her shoulders. "I did it on a reality TV show."

"Not funny."

"I'm not trying to be funny," she said, walking closer to him. She put her hands on his shoulders. "I love you too, but it feels crazy to say that after such a short time. I know that. I didn't want to scare you away."

"You're not scaring me away," he said, pulling her closer. "Please don't leave."

"So you're willing to be in a relationship with somebody who's going to be picked at on social media for all eternity?

Jack shook his head. "It's not going to last that long. People have very short attention spans, Ava. But I do need to know, are you interested in building a life with me?"

"Of course, I am," she said, pulling him into a tight embrace. Jack pulled back just enough to kiss her to seal the promise. It was a kiss that spoke of new beginnings, of forgiveness and acceptance. As they parted, they walked closer to the overlook, putting their arms around each other and staring out over the beautiful blue mountains. Jack had never felt so whole in his life. This was definitely going to be a challenge for them, but he knew that it was way more of a challenge to go back to that quiet cabin without Ava and Millie there.

"You know I have to get a place in town?" Ava said. "I can't just keep staying at your cabin."

"That's okay for now," Jack said.

"What is that supposed to mean?" she said, looking up at him laughing.

"I plan one day to have you and Millie with me forever."

"That sounds like a perfect plan."

Sometimes getting lost is the best way to find home.

EPILOGUE

$\mathcal{A}$va had gotten a cottage right in downtown Jubilee, a quaint little ivy-covered haven, just a stone's throw from the bustling square. The cottage had a cozy fireplace and a little garden out back, and it had quickly turned into a home. Jack enjoyed coming over and hanging out, and she enjoyed going to his cabin just as much. As they built their relationship, she couldn't imagine ever having a life without him. One day, she wouldn't rent this place anymore, but move to his cabin out in the woods, and they would continue building a life together. At least that's what she hoped. That's what they had talked about.

They dreamed of children running underfoot. Bonfires under the stars. Christmases by the fire.

Snowball fights in winter, playing in the creek in summer.

Jack, who once seemed so guarded, had now fully opened to all the love and light that Ava tried to bring into his life. He adored Millie, and they played together at the park often. He had taught her fetch, and she loved to swim in the local lake.

Together, they all explored the natural beauty that surrounded Jubilee. Hiking parts of the Appalachian Trail and walking along serene rivers and creeks. Their hikes had become almost a ritual, something that they did to keep their relationship alive, just like the surrounding landscape.

They had conversations about the future, about hopes and plans, and about their pasts. In the evenings, they would often return to his cabin or her cottage tired, but content, Millie at their feet as they sat by the fire talking and planning for the future.

They would walk to the square when they were at Ava's house and eat at the cafes or drink at the coffee shop. They would go on impromptu dates or just spend lazy afternoons walking around on the charming streets. Ava's cottage felt like a symbol of her new life. It was something that was just hers, and she was very proud of it. With Jack, she had found not just a partner, but a soulmate, someone who understood the shadows that lurked in her past and brought her light for their future together.

Her mom had even come to visit once, meeting Jack and falling in love with him. She realized he wasn't an axe murderer, and she was so happy Ava had found her person.

Thankfully, Jack had been right about social media. It hadn't lasted as long as she worried it would. People had already moved onto something else, namely the fact that Landon had already married another one of the contestants and they were pregnant with a baby boy. That kept people plenty busy online, and Ava's name rarely came up anymore.

She was glad because all she wanted to focus on was Jack and Millie. She had not just found a place to live in Jubilee, but a place where she belonged. She felt like she had endless possibilities for her future. She couldn't have been more grateful for that fateful day that she took a wrong turn and ended up on a snowy mountain because it led her to the place she could finally call home.

As the final rays of sunlight of the setting sun bathed Brady's new house in a warm golden glow, the anticipation was palpable. Tonight marked the culmination of not just months of hard work and planning, but the beginning of a new chapter in his life.

His house, which had once just been a blue-print on a piece of paper, now stood as a testament to the resilience of him and his family. Even though he had lost his childhood home to a fire months ago, this new one was ready to be filled with the same memories and laughter and warmth as the original one. The aroma of a hearty dinner wafted through the air in the open-plan kitchen, as Brady put the finishing touches on his famous meatloaf. The table was set with care by Madeline, each place setting an invitation to memory making.

As the doorbell rang, signaling the arrival of the first guests, Brady couldn't help but feel a surge of pride. Jack and Ava were the first to arrive, bottles of wine in their arms, and Ava handed them a home-made apple pie that she and Jack had made together. Their smiles were bright, their new love story well-known in town. Ava and Madeline had become good friends over the last few weeks, and Madeline was glad for it from what Brady could tell. She always needed more friends.

Eloise and Burt arrived together. They had been spending a lot more time at the park and at his home. Eloise was learning just how to feed the birds and the squirrels. They brought a big salad, and Eloise also brought something from the bakery.

More people arrived, including Clemmy, Lanelle, Heather and Ethan. Frannie and Cole were also on their way. Perky had a bit of a cold and couldn't make it, but promised to come see Brady's new home soon. Brady loved the feeling of a full house.

Anna was running around playing with Millie. Now that he had a house again, he thought about getting his own dog. Millie loved taunting Gilbert the goat when she was allowed outside in his area.

Geneva came and brought some homemade biscuits, which were something you had to have at every southern dinner get together. It just wasn't proper not to have biscuits.

They gathered around the table, the room lit up with not just the glow of the lights, but with the personalities sitting around the table.

"To new beginnings," Brady said, raising his glass. "And to this home that's finally not just complete, but full of cherished memories yet to be made."

Everyone said "cheers" and nodded as they began to eat. Brady looked around the table at all of these people that made up what he considered to be his family. Family wasn't just about blood. In fact, sometimes blood made absolutely no difference. It was about having people in your life who would be there for you, whether you were in the shadows or in the bright sunlight. People who would stand up, who would step up, who would defend you when you weren't around. Those were the kind of people that Brady wanted in his life. And as he looked around the table, all of these people were a testament to a life well-lived.

TO READ MORE Rachel Hanna books, go to store. RachelHannaAuthor.com and click on the READING LIST at the top!

Made in the USA
Middletown, DE
03 June 2024

55220471R00130